The White Lady
of
Marsaxlokk

ALSO BY ROSANNE DINGLI

Death in Malta
According to Luke
Camera Obscura
The Hidden Auditorium
Counting Churches – The Malta Stories
The Bookbinder's Brother
The Astronomer's Pig

Discover more about this author at:
www.rosannedingli.com

Acknowledgements

My infinite thanks go to Hugo Bouckaert, my first wise reader, without whom none of my novels would ever reach completion. I am also grateful to my squad of beta-readers, among whom Jon Kaneko-James and Becky Brandon went beyond the call of duty.

I acknowledge the work of a number of historians and photographers whose online depositories furnish not only material to the author, but also fact-checking facilities for the curious reader. The wealth of material available supports and enables research for my particular type of feasible fiction.

Author's use of facts

Turn to the back pages for a glossary and brief notes
on facts, history, and Maltese terms used in this novel

The White Lady
of
Marsaxlokk

Rosanne Dingli

Yellow Teapot Books
Australia

Rosanne Dingli © 2015

The right of Rosanne Dingli to be identified as the author has been asserted in accordance with sections 77 and 78 of the Copyright, Designs and Patents Act 1988. All rights reserved.

Yellow Teapot Books
Australia

ISBN-13: 978-1511622936

ISBN-10: 1511622938

This book is sold subject to the condition that it shall not, by way of trade or otherwise, be lent, resold, hired out or otherwise circulated without the publisher's consent in any form other than this current form and without a similar condition being imposed upon a subsequent purchaser.

Typesetting and cover design by *Ding!* Author Services
Author portrait by Mark Flower
Cover: Villa Sans Souci photograph by Werner Kuehn Koditek

This is a work of fiction. Names, characters, businesses, places, events and incidents, other than those clearly in the public domain, are the products of the author's imagination or used in a fictitious manner. Any resemblance to actual persons, living or dead, or actual events, is purely coincidental.

Contents

1 – Fragments of stone block *1*
2 – Rubble walls *10*
3 – Stony ground *21*
4 – The last marble tile *34*
5 – Strip of gravel *40*
6 – Bare stone *51*
7 – Winding staircase *60*
8 – Walled-up doors *67*
9 – Door jamb *74*
10 – Gazebo *79*
11 – Flagstones *86*
12 – Limestone building *93*
13 – Lodgings in Valletta *104*
14 – Green drawing room *108*
15 – Falling masonry *115*
16 – A wall niche *128*
17 – Bell arch *133*
18 – Glass door to the terrace *140*
19 – Double colonnade *147*
20 – Wiring and plumbing *155*
21 – Whitewash *160*
22 – Wooden window frames *171*
23 – Reconstruction *178*
24 – Plastic emulsion paint *182*

Author's use of facts *190*
Glossary *194*

One

Fragments of stone block

The doctor drove slowly to the beginning of the road, whose tarmac surface gleamed in the dying light. Just ahead, on the left, the house loomed, golden in the last rays of sunlight the day offered, after the afternoon's rain.

'This must be it.'

'It's a ruin, Philip.'

'But it's the one.' He stopped the engine and slowly got out of the brown rental Ford Escort. 'Villa Sans Souci, Marsaxlokk.' Something, he could not say what, caught him by the throat. He slid an old photograph from a jacket pocket. 'It's boarded up. Some of the masonry is missing. The bay windows and balconies seem to be crumbling, but look – the basic structure seems solid.'

'Solid?'

'It's solid, Meg. Substantial and salvageable, I think.'

'Oh, darling! You could not be thinking of ...' She moved forward from where she had tentatively emerged, close to the car, as if afraid to approach the building. She looked at the way loose blocks of stone were used to stop up doors and windows on the ground floor. 'It looks dangerous.'

'Everything we've seen today is *dangerous*. This whole island is risky. I mean ... tempting. Ever since we got off that ferry... Meg, can you see how different this place is? We've come all this way, down the entire Italian peninsula, all through Sicily, over the strait in a tin pot ferry, and now ... now, everything's in English. We had a perfectly good cup of tea, and real ham sandwiches, not an hour ago, in Rabat. Don't tell me you can't see any magic in this.'

Meg started to say something about tea and magic, but the doctor swung away, grey raincoat flapping in a breeze that came from somewhere behind her.

'I feel at home here. Aunty Claudia was right. I belong here.'

'Philip – you're Australian.'

He turned, his face dead serious. The frown lines on his forehead were prominent in the fading light. 'My people were Maltese. Decades ago, of course. But they were. I can't explain. It's just a feeling.' His arms rose and fell. Frustration pushed him forward.

'Where are you going?'

'I bet you can see the sea from the upper storeys.'

'Philip! You can't go in there. It's a ruin, I tell you.'

He walked alongside the limestone boundary, looking up at rusty iron railings in the wall. Before Meg could call out to him, Philip Falzon reached up and vaulted the railings in one smooth movement. His raincoat caught on one of the ornate spearheads and he heard it rip, but nothing could stop him. The narrow front garden was weedy and slippery after the rain. He stayed on a path of loose flagstones that led round the side, where he found a doorway stacked with loose rubble, some of it flaking, some of it grey like iron.

It was easy; he kicked at the bottom of the wall of rubble and it collapsed instantly, making him leap backward and nearly twist his ankle. He took a deep breath and avoided falling boulders and fragments of stone block. 'A way in.' He talked to himself. With Meg out of sight and out of earshot, he could do that. He could explore. Five minutes was all he wanted. Five minutes. Five minutes to absorb the atmosphere of that place. It was starting to enthral him. He needed to do it. It felt so … it felt like no other place he had ever visited.

But then, he did not break into abandoned ruins very often. This did not feel like intrusion. It felt like rediscovery. Unsteady on his feet, he stepped over rubble, rubbish; the accumulation of decades of debris, fallen from above. His eyes travelled upward as he entered a cavernous room without a ceiling.

'Oh god!' His exclamation rebounded off grimy walls full of half-hearted graffiti, gouges, spatters of paint, and the inexorable water stains that rain had channelled downward, through the broken roof, over the years. Grey, green, black.

He had seen nothing like this in his twenty-nine years. He had worked hard, he graduated, class of 1976, and did his internship, and was poised to start general practice. This holiday with Meg was necessary, urgent. He was practically exhausted. Newly married, on the verge of a new life. Exhausted. In seven weeks, however, when he was rested, when he had recovered, he would launch a career – a successful one, if hard work had anything to do with it.

Moving forward, he came into a huge space, once an enormous stairwell. 'Oh god!' Philip raised a protective arm over his head in realization that the entire staircase had collapsed at some point, making it possible for him to gaze upward to the sky from the ground level of this three-storeyed house. Two arched apertures and a Cyclops window loomed high above his head on the right. The day's last sun rays beamed in.

'Oh – what a pity. What a shame.' Words, words that came back at him, bounced off filthy walls. Dust, rubble, broken masonry and twisted metal rods and beams around him showed little evidence of glory or elegance, but he felt it was there once. 'The curved stairs are gone.'

They were gone, but the stubs of stone treads, some long, some shorter – the remnants of what once was a truly glorious staircase – were still embedded in the wall, curving upward, the bowed shape clearly outlined. He could see stone and plaster fragments banked and clinging to each stair stub, and traces on the wall of a painted green pattern, artfully done to resemble a trellis; a dado leading upward. 'The risers are gone, but parts of the treads are there. I wonder ...'

He could see others had tried before him, to the height of about ten stairs. The eleventh tread was piled with debris that had never been trodden or pushed aside. It was narrow and dangerous. Philip heard Meg's voice shout his name on the deserted road outside.

'Oh, *Meg!*' He mouthed exasperated words under his breath. She did not understand his feeling for this place. People said he was intuitive, an excellent doctor, with an instinctual bedside manner. He was spontaneous and fun to be with, his friends often said. But there was something deep inside him that had never been satisfied. Would climbing the remnants of those stairs give him part of what he sought, whatever it was?

Philip Falzon did not know. He did not understand what it was he sought, but he certainly had not found it yet. Meg's voice faded. She would wait. She had to wait. His foot found a clear space on the first tread, and on the second and third. Upward, he went upward, ascending towards a void. The stairs, he could now see, had led to a wide landing underneath a pair of ornate arches, joined in the middle by a fluted stone orb. What a glorious place this must have been once.

Now, it was a dump, a ruin. Meg was right. So why did it make him feel so welcome, so at home? The higher he rose, the more cautious Philip became. He did not dare look down. The rubble and wreckage that lay on the floor underneath him was ample proof that downward was the only direction solid matter travelled in that place.

His feet found space beyond the eleventh stair.

But it was clear no one had gone before him – not recently, in any case. Philip held his breath and climbed upward another nine treacherous treads, and came to a gap, fully three feet wide, in front of a platform composed of long limestone slabs, the remnants of wooden architraves and, dark brown with rust, some bent and twisted ancient metal beams. Rubble piled heavily everywhere. It was not a stable landing on a fine staircase any more. For some time, this had been a perilous perch, a full storey above ground level.

Philip waved away all thought of danger with his right hand. His left grasped a knob of stone that jutted out of the uneven wall. Deep audible breathing resounded in the cavernous space. 'Oh god. How will I ever get down again?' He dared not look down. The only way was forward, over that gap of empty space, underneath which, several metres below, was certain death. 'Oh god. I must be crazy.' He did not dare think what his weight might do to the landing if he jumped over that opening and landed heavily.

He held his breath and leapt.

'Oh.' He made it. 'Oh.' Righting himself where he landed, not daring to move another muscle, Philip waited. His ankle protested again. Would the whole structure collapse, taking it with him to the floor below?

It held, but it was not a safe perch. Knowing there was little underneath to support him, Philip looked up. The wall to his left was unusually marked. This was not the staining and blooming of green mould and rainwater runnels he had seen downstairs. This was not the grey, green and black of neglect. He wished he had more light. Peering into the darkness, he took two unsteady steps to the left and saw what it was.

A mural. A painting. A tracery of fresco. Imagery of a trellised garden, cleverly drawn so the perspective gave the impression of distance, of depth.

It was a wonderful garden, with arches of lattice bearing vines, some with blue blossom, others with white, fading into the distance where the landscape was golden. Church spires pierced the sky, which was a brilliant blue, studded with cotton-woolly clouds, and there, in the distance, a deep blue bay.

'How lovely. How beautiful and ...' Among the foliage, further on, Philip glimpsed movement. A minute, momentous, breathtaking miniscule movement. Could it be? No. No. A spark of white light. He held his breath. It was cold up here, it was suddenly freezing, but he did not dare move, lest whatever moved two seconds before would stop. Or pounce. Or escape. Or frighten him out of his wits with some unexpected action.

'Wait. Wait, wait. This is crazy.'

He heard something. Rustling. A footstep. No. It could not be. The rustling of some creature. Ah, a bird perhaps. Perhaps he disturbed some pigeons. It was the perfect place for pigeons, this ruin. But the mural ahead of him was ... no ... there it was again. A rustling sound coming from the wall ahead, from among the painted blue flowers; wisteria clumped, beautifully blue, among the green, in front of that golden landscape of distant buildings, sentinel churches, and faraway sea. How could a painted scene move?

Yes – he saw it again. A blink. An eyelid rapidly blinking. Then stopping. Where was it? Goodness. Just a flash, an instant. *What a beautiful face.*

Was that Meg's voice calling out on the road? No. Philip stopped breathing and listened. Someone else was breathing with him.

'Who's there?' His voice low, gentle, inquisitive. He did not feel foolish asking. Moving forward, his feet free now on something smooth, resonant, clean, supporting, he peered into brightening white light. And saw it again. A face, lovely eyes, a fringe of wavy brown hair. And pocked cheeks, now. Cruelly pocked and scarred cheeks.

His eyes tricked him. 'The mural is ruined.' His voice filled the space, which felt less open and echoing than before. 'Her face is ruined.'

A sudden intake of breath sounded.

Philip started back. He froze. He heard it. It was there. It was incredibly cold. He pulled his raincoat closer around him, knowing he had torn it on the fence. He felt for the ripped hem, but could not find the tear. Someone ahead, among the foliage of the garden mural, was breathing audibly.

'Who's there?'

'The paint is still fresh. Don't touch it. Papa said don't touch the wall.'

Philip's skin crawled. His heart leapt and beat so fast his breath caught in his chest. '*Who's there?*' He put out a hand and touched the wall, tentatively, ever so slightly, and looked at his fingertips, which held tiny dabs of fresh green and blue paint.

'I told you not to touch.'

'*What?* Who's there?' Fear clutched at Philip's chest. His hands and feet were frozen. He doubted he could move. But move he had to. Irresistibly, he inched backward, backward, feeling the soles of his shoes slither on the glossy surface of the marble floor. *Glossy?* He looked down, which was his undoing.

Falling, falling backward and outward, Philip's flailed his arms, seeking something, anything to hold on to. He clutched in thin air and grasped something, tearing a fingernail in an effort to break his fall. It was a stair tread. He embraced it, and swung his legs. He hung there, trying to remember where the other treads were, and how they were spaced. He tried to gauge how far it was to the ground. His heart beat audibly. His arms hurt. Groping at the wall, he found he could stretch to another tread, and hang from there. His feet found purchase on another stub of stone, and another, until it was safe to drop a few feet onto a pile of rubble.

'Philip! Philip?' Meg was still calling, outside.

'Stay there!' He yelled when breath returned to his chest in gulps. Circulation returned to his light head. His ankle hurt. His raincoat was ripped. 'Meg – stay where you are. I'm coming.'

It was pitch dark outside. He saw her silhouette at the end of the property. She was still on the road.

'What happened?'

'Meg ...'

'What happened? You were gone five whole *minutes.*'

Five minutes. It felt more like a week. A year. 'I've ... I need a torch.'

'You *are not* going back in there. Let's go. Come on, darling. It's pitch dark.'

Philip followed Meg out to the car, slipping twice in the loose rubble underfoot. 'We should come back. There's this glorious mural. You have no idea ...'

'Oh, really – whatever for? We have museums and galleries and lovely beaches and lots more to see. Besides – don't you want to look up some relatives you said you had addresses for?'

An impatient inhalation puffed up his chest. He let air out slowly. She was right. 'We must come back during the day and take photos, at least.'

'Oh, all right then. But I can't understand your fascination for this place.'

The man who had told him about it, sitting in a small café in Rabat, who had placed the old photograph on his table with a confident slap, seemed to think he would like it. Said he should take the photo.

'Go. You will like it.'

And he did. But the place was for sale, and some sort of commission might have been in the balance. Well, he had nowhere near anything Villa Sans Souci might be worth, ruin or no ruin. Besides, Meg was dying to return to Melbourne to start real life, whatever that meant to her as the young wife of a GP.

Perhaps they would have a young family, early. Who knew? Who could guess what the future held for them? He was starting to lose interest in the future, and ponder about the past.

'I heard something, Meg. I saw ...'

She laughed, pretty curls brushing the back of the car seat, gleaming in the dark. 'Let's go. I'm hungry and I want to change before dinner at the hotel. Floriana is so far away.'

'Nowhere's far away on this small island.'

'It is when you're hungry. Come on!' She laughed again. 'Of course you heard things. Pigeons kept coming, flying in from the fields and everywhere. I watched them, while you were inside. They probably nest there. You disturbed their home, Philip.'

'Yes, you're probably right.'

'You look a mess.'

'I broke a fingernail.'

She nodded. 'Serves you right, you silly man.' Her affectionate scolding sounded like she was smiling in the dark. 'You're crazy, trespassing like that in a condemned building.'

Trespassing? *Trespassing?* He did not think of it in that way at all. It all felt so much part of him. Of what he could be, of what he had once been. But when? Later, in the bright light of the hotel bathroom, he stared at his face in the mirror, and thought of another, more beautiful, face. A face ruined by pocks and pustules. A face damaged by the ravages of time on ancient plaster, of time on peeling paint.

Blue and green paint; fresh paint, still sticky, ingrained into the whorls of the skin on his index and middle fingers. He put them under his nose. Fresh, fresh, smelling of turpentine and spirit. Linseed oil and pigments.

*

Two

Rubble walls

The professor was driven along the road. He adjusted his glasses, smoothed his moustache and beard, looked past the leather curtain of the small carriage, and considered the loose surface, the need for more gravel to be strewn, or perhaps tarring of the road. The horse's hooves clattered in the still night.

In this darkness, with the carriage lantern eerily illuminating only as much thoroughfare as they could traverse in two or three minutes, it felt like the end of the world. Installation of gas street lights had reached Rabat, and even part of the long road to Verdala. But here, at the south-eastern tip of the island, approaching the crooked bay from the last town, it was not far from being a wilderness. A dark, gently undulating wilderness of carob trees and vines.

The last town, Żejtun, was brilliant with light. The forecourt of the enormous church seemed flooded with lantern light on the eve of the feast day of St Catherine of Alexandria. Candles, gas, spirit and kerosene lamps, and oil in sconces with sheep-wool wicks were not stinted on, for such an evening. He came away reluctantly, but knew he would be heartened by lights at the windows of his own distant house.

What had possessed him to build such a mansion in such a place? The question only lived in his head for an instant. It was peaceful, peaceful here among the olive groves and the vineyards. His own land, bounded by high rubble walls, the kind called by the people *tas-sejjieh*, extended far beyond the road, and Marsaxlokk Bay was less than two miles to the east, so fresh fish was abundant, brought to the house still wriggling in a basket.

His coachman too was eager to reach the house.

The retainer's family, who served at the house, lived in tidy quarters next door. He had even seen to, and paid for, the building of a shrine to St Joseph in their courtyard, which led to the fields behind the formal garden of the house. What abundance of tomatoes, figs, onions and aubergines were had in the summer; what a number of baskets of marrows and plums. And the servants and their children thrived on watermelon and prickly pears. In the winter, there were blood oranges and tiny mandarins with loose skin, from the small grove at the back. It was heaven, he supposed; a kind of heaven. Still, there was a sense of dread in his stomach as the horse clip-clopped around the bend.

He heard his own rapid intake of breath. For an instant, for less than a minute, the doctor's eyes were tricked by the gloom. To his sight, the house appeared a ruin. Masonry had fallen to the road. The windows on the ground floor seemed blind, empty, robbed of the beautiful wooden shutters he had ordered with such care. Where were the wrought-iron balconies? Where were the carefully tended white-flowering oleanders? What happened to the bell arch he had installed for use in emergencies – what *happened*?

This could not be ... in the domed darkness of one of the upstairs windows, he glimpsed a wraith, a white form like a veiled figure. His heart stopped, but only for an infinitesimal moment. The coach lamp's glow lit up the road ahead, and the doctor shook his head.

An ache started at the base of his neck and travelled up, up and around to his brow. No, no. Everything was fine; there was his house, with lights glowing in the windows upstairs. Marianna made sure, if he was not home by dark, that lamps were lit in the windows to welcome him home, lamps he could see from a distance.

Tonight, something tricked his eye. Tonight fate showed him something awful; a vision of deterioration that came with time. Who knew what would happen to his glorious mansion? It was designed with such care and deliberation. He had sat for hours with the architect, whose constant sniffs, and scratching with a graphite pencil on those large plans, were so annoying.

He had endured such painful impatience waiting for the arrival of materials from the docks at Marsa. Marble from Italy. Timber from Sicily and Greece. Glass from Czechoslovakia and England. Then he had to take on an English engineer to make sure artisans and workmen were employed who could follow precise instructions. Finally, after five years endured living with his cousin's family in Valletta, it was completed, and he moved in. Weeks later he installed his household.

He remembered walking Marianna through the estate, listening to her plans for further decoration and embellishment of the many rooms. She wanted damask drapes, blinds brought from the Low Countries, rugs from Persia, muslin bed hangings from Prague for their tiny daughter. And a bell of handsome bronze from Belgium, cast to sound a pure note. It arrived, and was suspended from the arch on the roof. The coachman made sure the metal cable let into the wall worked well. The doctor tried it. Once. *Dong.* The bell rang, clear and round. Its hum was a perfect tonic *la.*

'A beautiful sound.' Marianna tilted her head toward the hum. 'It seems perfect for emergencies. You are inspired. It's a pity we will hear it rarely, or never at all.'

'It was your idea, my dear.' He had looked at her, this beautiful intelligent woman, whom people had labelled *inappropriate*, and a *vulgar choice*. How dare they judge? It was true, she was an actress, and born on the volcanic island of Stromboli, but her poise and elegance, her taste and knowledge of the works of playwrights since Aeschylus was tremendous. What would they know of her? She was magnificent, and had deigned to marry him, almost in secret, almost furtively. He had regrets now, about such a hurried stealthy wedding – she was worthy of a ceremony that brought out crowds to look upon her, but it was done now. They had nothing to hide. And living far away from the gossiping crowds would raise their union from gossip fodder to elegant mystery.

The sky looked ominous now. There was a bank of menacing cloud, curving and curling on the horizon over the bay. The doctor knew he could not see the sea from the road, so only looked at the bright lining of the clouds, clouds, which cheered him inside as they parted to reveal the moon. Not a full moon, but very nearly, and it lit up the landscape as if to guide him safely home. He heard the coachman laugh.

'*Dak qamar*!'

'Yes, Karist – it surely is a remarkable moon. And cheering, in this darkness. We are home.'

Karist sounded the carriage bell, a thin metallic ping, two rings, and someone opened the *remissa*.

Yes, they were home at last, and all visions of a ruined home, of masonry falling to the ground, of railings twisting and rusting, of vandals and thieves running off with sections of marble and lengths of damask, of robbers escaping with parts of his precious ivory collection, evaporated as voices from the house sounded in the quiet of the fields at night.

The doctor shivered as he alighted from the carriage and stood under the small portico. The hallway was ablaze with light. A few paces, and he saw her, at the top of the stairs. All the servants had disappeared to their quarters.

'You made good time?' Marianna looked splendid, but tired. She never retired before he came home.

'It's very late.' They spoke in Italian to each other. Maltese was reserved for the servants and tradesmen. Some people in the towns beyond Valletta spoke nothing but English, but that was to be expected. Those suburbs were crowded with the military. His own English was more than just good, and he often translated medical papers from one language to another.

He looked up and continued, wanting to impress her with how he felt as he came up their road. 'The darkness was appalling. The moon came out at the very last minute.' He looked at her, all in yellow, framed by the twin arches in the stair well. She lit up the house like a lamp.

The blank wall behind her, large, square and cream in colour, needed adornment. He had an idea which cheered him further as he ascended the fine stairs. 'Marianna, I've just had a thought. What if we got Lazzaro to paint a mural on the wall behind you?'

She turned, her silk dress swishing audibly. 'Oh, yes. Oh yes, Luigi! Lazzaro is just the right person. What do you think it should be? A *trompe l'oeil*?'

He laughed at the way she immediately understood what he meant. 'In a way. You know how we love the view from the side terrace, over the fields and gardens, down to the bay? Well, we could get Lazzaro to repeat that view here.' He held up a hand and placed it flat on the wall. He did not say to her; *So when it's night outside, and frightfully dark, we would always have a sunlit scene in here.*

She nodded. 'Splendid – then we could have the pleasing landscape all around us. On the terrace to the left, and on the wall to the right. How lovely.'

'Are you sure you would not prefer a scene from the *Commedia dell'Arte* ... or perhaps something from Shakespeare or Molière?'

'How sweet you are.' Her sweet laugh tinkled and resounded on the banister and landing railing. 'No, Luigi. A garden scene would be the most elegant, appropriate, and pleasing to us both.'

'I shall write to him in the morning.'

'So your plans for a gazebo ...?'

He gave her a tired but loving smile. 'You love those plans. You yearn for shelter in the garden. Even I can anticipate small gatherings you will have there, and little picnics with Prasseide. The foundations for the gazebo will start right away.'

Marianna clapped her hands like a child.

'How is our pretty daughter?'

'Asleep, of course. Lieni took her up a bit early today. She did love it when someone brought white grapes in from across the vineyards.'

'Good. Good. I must say one thing. Stay close to home. Do not enter the towns for a while. Stay here and visit the bay. Tell the boy to take you down in the small garry, with the young pony. There is an outbreak of smallpox in Valletta. You do know how dangerous it is. It maims. It scars. It's lethal.'

'Smallpox!'

'It comes on the ships, my dear. On the ships. It takes hold in seaside towns, starting at the wharves. Stay here, you and Prasseide.'

'I would never place us at risk.'

'I know you would not.'

Lazzaro Pisani lived with them for three months. 'I could not have done the painting, such a large mural, if I had to travel back and forth, back and forth all the time. Do you know how long it takes to get here from Valletta?'

'My dear man – of course I know. Was I not given a stipend from the Health Department just for the reason of distance? I employ a coachman and have a specially-made carriage.'

'Why you came out here is beyond me.'

The doctor laughed. 'Beyond you ... and beyond all noise and disturbance. Beyond the reach of diseases, which flow off those ships like the plague.'

Lazzaro crossed himself. 'Do not court fate by mentioning *that*!'

The doctor laughed again. 'You refused the commission twice. I almost had Calì up here, showing me designs for that wall.'

'That Neapolitan charlatan! What does he know?'

'Hardly a charlatan. And they say he has a very talented son.'

The artist lowered his repentant head and eyed the decanter. 'May I?' He poured himself another glass when the doctor nodded. 'Well – I hope you did not consider having a child of ten paint you such a complex mural. Look – I'm here now. I intend following the roof cove, with an arch ...' He took a pencil from his breast pocket, and a scrap of paper, and sketched as he spoke. '... like this. And then have, in the foreground, a tracery, a structure, similar to the metal and wood pergola you have on the terrace ...'

'A bower, yes. All you have so far, however, is a reddish background. I cannot imagine anything, you know. Not even Marianna can look at a red wall and see a landscape.'

The artist sketched some more. 'Look, look – the red is just surface preparation. What do you want, for the fresco to crumble and fade in a year?'

The artist's sketch seemed to make sense. He certainly had a way with perspective. There, on his own dining room table, on a yellowish scrap of paper, the doctor could see his own pergola on the side terrace, draped and strung with creeping vines and climbing roses. Beyond were fields and houses, with spires and steeples in the distance. Then, a few horizontal lines and pencil curves described the sea and clouds on the horizon.

'Yes, yes – we have countless sketches of yours showing this marvellous view. The coloured one you made for Marianna is simply delightful. But when will we start to see more than just a flat red background?'

'In a few days the green goes on. And some blue. I need a boy to help stir the paint and hold the ladder.'

'The coachman has three sons.'

'No, no – no, Luigi. I need the boy who's helped me before. He knows to hold the ladder properly. He knows how to place the supports when I need to rest my arm. He holds the palette just at the right angle. It took me months to teach him. He can sleep in my dressing room.'

'No. No! He will have to lodge with the servants.'

'Of course! He will be on his way from Floriana tomorrow, I think.'

The doctor tilted his head. 'It's arranged, then.'

'Everything. Everything.'

Luigi's dream recurred. It was a nightmare that made him sit upright in bed, muttering gibberish. His nightshirt was bunched around his waist, his pillow a lumpy mess.

Marianna turned in the dark. 'Shall I light ...'

'Yes. Light a candle. Light. Light! A lamp. Two lamps. I had the dream again. Show me *where I am*.'

The flare of a struck match was enough.

'Ah! *Għall-erwieħ!*'

'What?'

The doctor lay back on his pillow. 'It's all right, Marianna. I do not have to speak in Italian all the time.'

It was not that. He had uttered the equivalent of a prayer. It was not like him. She gathered the light fabric of her nightgown around her, and perched on the end of the bed closer to her beset husband. 'I mean, Luigi – why are you praying and uttering exclamations like an old man, in the middle of the night?'

'It's nothing.' He raised an arm and buried his face in the elbow.

'This *nothing* that has you beleaguered like this is a very big *nothing*. Three times this month you have woken up shivering and shaking from *nothing*.'

He bit the flannel of his night shirt, and rolled his haggard eyes.

'You're afraid of something. This dream is more than you say it is.'

'Oh, Marianna – you know I do not like the dark.' He regretted the words, so he added some more optimistic ones. 'The mural is nearly finished.'

She shook her head. 'What do you mean? That can't be it. You are paying Lazzaro handsomely. Everything is fine. It's a pleasant thing. What do you mean?'

He had to tell her, but what would he say that explained this foreboding, this feeling of dread? 'There is smallpox in Marsa. In Rabat.' He lied. He lied to her about the reasons behind his fear, in the middle of the night.

'Hm, I know. That boy Lazzaro has employed ... he did not look too well, so I got Karist to take him away, back to his family.'

The doctor sat upright again. 'What!'

'The boy. The painter's boy. He was sick.' Marianna tried to soothe him. 'Let me get you something to drink.'

'Sick!' He swung his legs over the side of the bed. 'Even if I drink the entire contents of the cellar, even if I gulp down the entire Mediterranean *Sea*, Marianna, it will not reverse what might have happened.' He did not bother to thrust his feet into slippers; the doctor marched across the bedroom barefooted, and wrenched open the door to the landing, walked hurriedly across, eyes averted from the mural. 'She stands by and watches while Lazzaro paints. Our daughter. Every day!'

'Luigi ...!'

'And the boy is there, stirring paint! A sick boy ... holding the ladder ... carrying the pox!'

Marianna heard him waking their daughter.

'Prasseide! Prasseide!' And then a forceful, miserable groan. 'It's too late! It's too late ...'

'What is it, Luigi?' Sorrow, regret, and a thousand other emotions forced Marianna's question into a mangled croak. Their daughter lay awake, her eyes rolling from ceiling to wall, from her father's face to her mother's.

'Prasseide ...'

She was running a fever, and her face was blotched and discoloured.

'It's nothing, a cold perhaps.'

He placed a hand under his daughter's chin. 'Nothing! It's a high fever. Where does it hurt, my sweet? What ...?'

'My back hurts, my back.'

The doctor hung his head. Ragged nightmarish breath racked his chest. His life would never be the same again. He buried his face in his hands. 'My daughter. My beautiful daughter. Oh.' The recurring dream came to him once more, as he sat there, distraught. His daughter's hot fist grasped his nightshirt.

Marianna needed an answer. 'What is it, Luigi?'

'I dreamed the mural was ... every few nights, I dreamed it went back to a flat red-painted wall. Every morning I woke to see Lazzaro's progress. The wisteria, the trellises, the sea in the distance under those clouds ...' It was the truth at last.

'Luigi!'

'And every second night, in my head, before my dreaming eyes, it went back to red... red ... flat, nothing.'

'Papa, it hurts.' Prasseide turned her head sideways and vomited all over her pillow.

'Call Lieni. Wake everyone up.' He lifted his daughter out of the bed, even if repulsed by the smell of her vomitus. 'We must nurse this child back to health. We must do everything we can.' He lay her in an armchair, and wiped her face with a towel his wife handed him. 'Bring hot water.' He lowered his head and thought hard. 'Bring cold water. Fill the slipper bath. Have the bath brought in here, and get Lieni and the others to fill it.'

'A bath! In cold water! She will catch her death.'

'Hush. *Hush*, I tell you. I know what to do.' He turned to the child. 'We'll help you. I'll help you. I'm a doctor, my sweet – I know what to do. I'll be by your side. I shall never sleep again. I'll never see that red wall again.'

*

Three

Stony ground

Philip Falzon drove slowly to the beginning of the road in the rented Hyundai. It was the same, and yet it was not. The fields on either side were well-cultivated, lined with grapevines. The traffic was not heavy, but it was there, unlike on the previous occasion, years ago, when he had driven there before.

Alone now, he was; but rather than lonely, he felt a piercing wave of anticipation and strange confidence enfold him. Yes, there it was. There it was still. The house loomed as he came through a bend in the road. The years had not treated it kindly. A lot of the beautiful masonry that had decorated the façade was gone, either in a deliberate action by whoever had widened and bituminised the road, or through simple erosion that dropped blocks of limestone earthward, to shatter and crumble on the stony ground.

The apertures were now fully stopped up by remnant blocks of the same stone. The railings were gone. The memory of a ripped raincoat hem suddenly came to him, and he fumbled in the car, touching the hem of his jacket. That rip was a complete mystery. He had kept that raincoat for years. It was badly ripped, but his mind went back to how he had climbed what was left of the stairs, and how there was no rip as he stood and gazed at what remained of that mysterious mural. Then, when he sought the hem of the coat back in the car with Meg, it was there again, fraying already; a new coat ruined.

The spearhead railings were gone, and so were the decorative wrought-iron balcony rails. All the windows were flat and blind. 'Oh, oh – my beautiful house. What has happened to you?'

What had happened to Philip Falzon in the intervening years could not be seen on his person. His face too stayed unlined and youthful, but his heart had hankered to be here, to return to this house, which had haunted his mind the entire twenty-five years. Now, with his practice safely operating without him, his family grown, his wife engaged in community work, he could travel on his own, all the way around the globe, and seek what he always sought. He could not always vocalize what it was he wanted, but alighting from that plane that day gave him the initial shivers of a sensation he had not felt since his honeymoon with Meg on that tiny island.

'I'm back. I'm back, house.' He addressed the ruin as if it could hear him. Disappointment at its deterioration overwhelmed him for a moment, coming close to quashing the pleasure he had felt to hear it was still there, still crumbling, still on the market. For sale? Who would enter such a ridiculous contract?

'Oh, it's been bought and sold again, in the past fifteen years, but no one has touched it. No one has done anything to halt the destruction of time.'

Elaborate words from a real estate agent. 'I take it you are interested, sir?' He pushed forward a business card.

'I shall let you know. Is this your number? I'll let you know.' Philip fended off the hard sell and made off to the house, to survey what the years had wreaked. This, in his home slang, was a bulldozer job. Worth nothing but the land it stood on. And even that seemed to have shrunk in size. Farmers on all three sides had known how to inch and shave slivers off over the years, moving fences, planting prickly pear, until it was a mere asymmetrical rhomboid of rubble and thicket, nothing close to its previous breadth and width.

He walked on the road outside, displeased at the traffic that zoomed past, at the white dust that was greyer near the roadside, at the inclement sun that drummed down on the white stone, grey stone, pink and yellow stone. Stone everywhere, stopping up doorways and windows, forming an impassable barrier. How could anyone walk in now? It was impossible to walk on, all that large rubble, composed of fragments of stone blocks and wedges of limestone. There were brown twisted beams and lengths of bent metal rods. There were the leavings of decades, right at his feet.

This time, he had a ladder; a telescopic aluminium thing that was light and expensive, bought in Rabat and still bearing the price sticker. Useless. It would probably prove useless, and getting it inside would be well-nigh impossible. There would be nowhere to stand it. Why did he arrive in the afternoon? He should have risen earlier and come in the morning, but things kept getting in his way. Time was not a constant thing on this island, as it was in his clinic. Time was made of more elastic stuff here. It was made of dust and sunlight and inexorable traffic; the push of crowds. People, people, all wanting to do the same thing at once.

He looked up at the façade. Where was the glory and potential he saw there, twenty-five years ago? It was all gone. The arch where a bell once hung was broken, probably struck by lightning. It still stood, its lopsided stone form tempered to a steely grey. Limestone was like that; it either stayed pink and crumbly, or hardened to a density that was impermeable, eternal. It was why old buildings were so vulnerable, and only as long-lasting as their weakest blocks and roofing slabs. He had heard this from the mouth of the pushy real estate agent, a few hours ago. He called roofing slabs *xorok*, in the local building vernacular. For Philip, that word initially had no meaning, but now, peering through the upper storey blind window apertures at what was left of this house's roofing, open to the skies, the word *xorok* started to mean something. If a house was to endure, its roofing slabs and beams had to bear the stresses of time and climate.

And the climate here was deceptive. Sunny Malta, they called it, but no one could deny the viciousness and brute strength of Mediterranean storms that lashed at the rocky island. No one could refute the certainty of the arrival of tempests, winter after winter, to lash at rock-solid houses, whose stone blocks, hewn out of the very bedrock they all lived on, frequently, and with the erosion of time, rendered them vulnerable. An unoccupied house, without the eternal vigilance of its owners, could start to crumble in a decade.

Leaving the folding ladder where it was in the car, Philip moved forward, impatient to renew his acquaintance with the interior. But he could see no way in, even though the wall and its metal railings were long gone. He remembered the sound of fabric ripping when he tore his raincoat on those railings, as he walked the length of the façade. There was still a passage down the side, impenetrable for heaps of rubble and the remnants of a boundary wall. It was easy to scale this mound, and the marks and tracks of previous shoe soles told him he was not the first to come that way. 'Here I go.'

A bank of fluffy cloud temporarily hid the sun and Philip experienced a sharp shiver across his shoulders, and a melancholy peal – a single note – reached his ears from above. *The bell.* A single clang from the bell; a bell that no longer existed, that no longer hung in that ruined arch, three storeys above his head. Surely, his mind was playing tricks on him. His feet moved onward, while his head and heart filled with a feeling he had not had for twenty-five years. Was it foreboding or was it part of him? Did it fill him with dread, or a sense of homecoming?

His head told him he did not belong here, to turn around and return to the car. But he would fight the rationale. Something else flooded in to stop him acting reasonably, and he kicked and pushed with unwonted force against a walled-up doorway.

In exactly the same way it had so many years in the past, the obstacle fell, crumbling and crashing to his feet, so he had to take a startled pace backwards. 'A way in.' He was inside, where he expected to find the same debris, the same rubbish and accumulations of years. But the inside hallway was now clear. The fragments had been piled into two of the corners, which made the space seem even larger than he remembered.

The bell rang again. One disconsolate peal. He listened to its diminishing hum. Philip wished he were a musical person, able to tell what note it was. In his head, recognition of that sound was immutable. Undeniable. He knew what it meant. But how could he? Taking a few steps backward, he peered upward, upward into what was left of the light of the day, to try and discern whether the back wall of the landing ... yes. The mural was still there. Twenty-five years had not taken away any of its mystery. His skin crawled. His breath quickened. There were even less of the stair-tread stubs now than when he had first climbed to that level. And he was a much younger man then. The memory of how he had nearly fallen from above made him shiver.

The ladder in the car, he guessed, would only take him as far up as the eleventh or twelfth stair. Two more paces back, without looking where he trod, and his casual synthetic lace-ups squeaked on fine marble underfoot. White, polished marble tiles with grey veins, and looking around, a border of patterned tiles showing an unusual Greek key design. Clean, gleaming in the half-light. *Clean.* He dared not look up, lest the floor returned to what it was when he entered – gravelly, piled with dust and loose mortar, stacked in the corners with shattered plaster and blocks of broken masonry.

The smell in his nostrils was no longer what Philip associated with disused buildings; rat-nest stink, human urine, air-borne dust, ancient mortar. No. No.

He smelled something like the lure of sandalwood; something like the scent of incense. He smelled perfume. He dared not raise his eyes, or it would be gone. In his ears there was nothing but swishing of branches against the walls outside. Nothing but rustling of something silken, something like a woman's skirts muffling her footfall. The hairs on the back of his neck rose, and fear clutched at his stomach. He heard the bell once more. Once. One lonely peal. He decided it was A, the note A. Clear, an absolutely pure sound. A sad sound, one that tore at his head. His throat tightened. If it sounded again, it would bring him to tears. He dared not raise his eyes. Somewhere above, someone waited. Waited.

Patient enough to see how long it took before he raised his eyes, someone waited. It chilled his hands and feet. It was June, the end of a sunny June afternoon outside, and yet his limbs froze. He felt an icy sensation inch up his spine. He was cold, and still did not dare raise his eyes. The memory of a beautiful face came to him. *What a beautiful face.*

Then he remembered the ravages of whatever had pocked that face. Was it a painted face in the mural, ruined by time, deteriorated by rain, graffiti, and the imperfections of an ill-prepared and plastered wall? Was it a face withered by some disease that covered the victim with pustules? All he remembered was his feeling. It crept around him again.

This time, Meg was not outside, waiting for five minutes near the car. This time he was alone, with his new ladder in the parked car, with no time limit except that exerted by sunset and descending darkness. His torch was thankfully in his pocket. He patted his jacket and his heart shrank again. No torch. His feet, clad in highly polished dark leather, his trouser legs, clad in some sort of black gabardine, his knees, shaking slightly, were all he could see above the gleaming marble floor. *Leather? Gabardine?* He dared not look up. Looking up would erase all this. It would fling him back unwillingly to the reality of a house falling down among its own remains. A house in ruins.

He waited for the bell to ring again. He took a deep breath, to once more savour that heady scent of sandalwood. Deep breathing, head down. He could not stay like this forever.

'*Non sale?*'

The words echoed in the space, and chilled Philip to the core. A female voice, but powerful. He recognized the language; Italian. He knew just enough to understand opera lyrics, so he saw she asked, very formally, whether he was not going to ascend. Was he to go up?

To his surprise, he uttered a one-word response in Italian. '*Salgo.*' I'm coming up, he said to the voice. Did he have no control over his own words? 'I'm coming.'

Freezing, chilled to the bone, Philip started for the stairs, laid his right hand on the banister, and started up. There was a central chandelier that sparkled to his right, a fretwork of green *tromp l'oeil* trellis to his left. His leather-soled shoes clattered on the stair treads.

'You are very late. I have waited several hours.'

'I'm coming up.'

'You do know how impatient I get.'

When could he raise his eyes? He dared not look up. He watched his feet ascend, stair by stair, following the curve of the flight. Half way up, he stopped. 'May I look up?' This was new deference, for him.

Her laughter rang in the space exactly as another peal rang out from the bell above their heads. Both sounds chilled his chest.

She stopped. 'Can you imagine how the ringing of that bell terrifies the peasants?'

'It frightens me.'

'So it should. You do well to arrive just before

sunset. And no, no – you may not. You may only look up when you reach my side.' She moved. There was a rustle of lace or tulle or muslin, barely audible, and he knew she was pulling a veil over her face. He knew, he knew. How could he possibly know?

I am Philip Falzon, he wanted to say. 'I have kept you waiting, I am so sorry,' came out of his lips, in Italian. His left hand reflexively rose to his lips. What was he saying? 'Um... will it ring again? I find it ...'

'It is the bell of dread. It is supposed to summon help, but all it does is strike fear into the hearts of the peasants. Only nearby field workers can hear it. Oh, and perhaps the occupants of the Villa Marnisi across the vineyards. But they will not hurry. They will send a coachman, at best. They are too terrified to help.'

'To help?' His feet stopped. He was somewhere in the middle of the flight. At the eleventh stair. 'To help with what?'

'Pain. Pain and tears. Disease. Death. Abandonment.'

'Mi ricordo di un volto perfetto.' Philip touched his lips again. What was he saying? 'I remember a beautiful face.' That was what he said, and he did remember it among the foliage, on that freshly painted wall. The girl had asked him not to touch it, and he went away with paint on his fingers.

'My face was perfect once. No one can now bear to look at me. Come up. See if you are the only one who can bear to gaze upon ... to see what I really look like.'

Philip climbed all the stairs and gazed downward at the hem of a dark green dress, the toe of a black shoe. His eyes climbed the length of the gathered skirt, past the tightly belted waist, a rounded bodice, a scooped neckline of stiff lace, and skin. The ravaged skin of neck and throat, before the veil was lowered again, swiftly, to hide everything; neck, throat and face covered by a film of black muslin.

'I dress like a widow, you see.'

'I see.'

'I leave this house only in a carriage, behind a curtain, with an ancient coachman who has never seen my face, lest I scare him away, and be left completely alone, with no one. Deserted servants' quarters – what a horrible thought. No one to ... to run the house. That is a destiny worse than death.'

Her words were like poetry, like opera lyrics; Philip understood every word, and was chilled by his understanding. 'Than death,' he repeated, feeling foolish. Feeling out of control. 'I am ... I feel like a marionette.'

She laughed. 'That is what you always say. Please follow me.'

Always? When had he talked to her before? Always? A breeze out of nowhere, a bitter draught, caught him in the face. He blinked, blinded, confused for a moment, and there it was, fresh and vivid; the mural on the back wall of the landing. It was brilliant. Philip felt he stood on a terrace looking out over fields and groups of houses and churches all the way to the sea, through clumps of blue and white wisteria. 'Always beautiful.'

'So you say. Follow me.' She climbed a flight upward, stopping at a painted metal gate and opening a complicated lock. Forward she went, with Philip behind her. There was a second gate, which she opened with a second key, found hanging from her waist on a long chain. 'Do you know what would happen if these keys were lost? They were lost once, and the whole household did not rest until they were found.'

'But they *were* found. In the gazebo.' How did he know? How did those words leave his lips?

The room they entered was ablaze with candlelight. No; gaslight, from three chandeliers, whose flames were protected by etched bowls, flutes, nozzles and lids. They illuminated a chamber so beautiful Philip had to stop and take it in. His body was frozen, his feet barely functioned. His spine tingled and was struck numb with the cold, but he looked around to take in the mesmerizing quality of the room's decoration.

'Come on.' She urged him forward. 'Do not act like it's the first time you have entered this room.'

Everything, very nearly everything, was green and glimmering gilt. She formed part of her surroundings, dressed in a complimentary dark green shade. Upholstery, drapes, and carpet were immeasurably luxurious. The paintings in gilt frames, mostly circular and oval, were greenish in character; landscapes and gardens of hypnotic excellence. Nothing was shrouded in black but her face.

'You would think we might have no mirrors in this unfortunate house. But we do.' Her upturned palm indicated a series of tall thin rectangular mirrors, each in an ornate gilt frame, hanging between those heavily curtained windows. If Philip had the presence of mind to count them, he would have found three on each side. If he had the courage to look, he would have seen her form reflected many times around the room, and no reflection of his.

He inhaled deeply, the frozen air hurting his nostrils, throat and lungs. The brilliant scent of sandalwood entered his head, seeped to the spaces behind his eyes and nose. He would faint if he did not sit down.

She waved him to a gilt and green damask sofa, and he could finally lean back and stretch his legs in front of him. Automatically, reflexively, with the habit of decades, his fingers pulled at the creases in his perfect trousers, and undid a breast button so his well-tailored jacket would not crease. He smoothed the front of his silk shirt, and knew to refrain from touching his bowtie. *Tie it perfectly and it will stay perfect.* Whose words were those?

Somewhere in the dim recesses of his head, a mother paced, a father gazed. Whose – his? It could never be. Philip Falzon lost both his parents to a highway accident when he was only eleven. They were crushed by a road grader. He was crushed by having to live with Aunty Claudia, no matter how well-meaning and gentle she was.

'Prasseide ...' How did he know her name?

'No matter how far and wide you all search, you will never find me a husband. What do you think you are, some kind of marriage broker?' She spat the word out viciously, in Maltese. *'Ħuttab? Ħuttab?'*

Philip saw that her use of the language was no compliment. She was treating him like a servant. The choice of language was a choice of mood, of direction, of consideration. It was a social insult. Part of him did not mind. Another part, his sensitive, intuitive self, was flooded with sorrow, with pity, with a frightening kind of grief and melancholy he could not remember ever experiencing. Something in his bones told him what would happen.

The bell sounded. One strike, a perfect note; A, somewhere above them. 'That bell.'

'La campana di Papà.'

'Father's bell?'

'Do you pretend not to remember his remorse? His gentleness? His infinite wisdom and sorrow?' She had beautiful hands, pale and narrow. Identical diamond rings graced the middle finger of each, and if Philip stared, which he did, he could see the back of each hand was cruelly scarred and blemished. She raised one hand and pulled back the veil.

Philip inhaled swiftly. His choked breath was audible in the room. His own gelid hands clasped and came loose again, and reclasped. 'Your face.'

Beautiful eyes stared out of lined and cratered skin. Her lips were still beautiful, even if her teeth behind them were uneven and distorted. Her cheeks were rutted areas of dents and lines, craters and pustule scars. 'My face,' she repeated in Italian. 'Pretty Prasseide's face. Ruined at the age of twelve. *She lived, she lived,* they cried. But I died the day that painter's apprentice came to this house. *Do not touch the mural,* they said. I did not. I touched nothing. I did nothing. I watched that mural appear out of a flat red wall. As it took shape, as the clouds and trellises and wisteria took their lifelike forms ... as they took life, I died.'

The words were not angry or vicious now. Philip looked at her eyes, only at her eyes. He ignored the gouged ravaged flesh around them and gazed into her eyes.

'The boy brought ...'

'He brought disease to the house. To me. Only to me. And now they wish to marry me off.'

'I am no marriage broker.'

'What are you then, Philip?' She knew his name. How did she know his name?

Philip tried to rise to his feet but found he was immobile. He tried again. 'You mistake me for someone else.' His heels slid ineffectually on the fine silk rug, whose pattern was mesmerizingly engaging. From her face to the floor, his gaze passed, and back, and back again. To the rug, the green patterned rug. Dizzy with shock and cold, he could do nothing but sit back, and wait for the weakness to pass.

The doctor was woken by the single ring of a bell somewhere above him. The melancholic note diminished to a hum and stopped. He looked up, although he knew he would see little. It was a reflexive movement to the sound, a reaction that seemed irrepressible. He saw the sky, black and streaked with visible grey cloud. His back hurt. The rubble on which he lay was rough. It threatened to slit his clothes. Not far from his left hand a twist of rusty metal vibrated to the sound of something.

'*La,*' his lips said. He raised a hand to his mouth. '*La,*' he said again. He could not stand one moment longer in this house. It was getting dangerous. '*Do ... re, mi, fa, so, la. La ... la.*'

Rubble could plummet to where he lay any second. Whole blocks of stone could fall and shatter on the rough ground that was ruining his jeans. He came to his feet slowly, arching his spine. How long had he lain there? To his left, the doorway he had kicked free of old smashed masonry gaped, filled with night and the noises of swishing branches. A stiff breeze from Marsaxlokk Bay drove litter and dead foliage inside. It fluttered and rustled.

He was in his rental Hyundai very quickly, his legs pumping with more energy than he felt. 'The sooner I'm under my hotel shower, the better.' Talking to the rear-view mirror seemed less insane than what he remembered of the afternoon.

*

Four

The last marble tile

The professor stood on the terrace in the evening, the glow of his ignored cigar becoming brighter as the day came to an end. From the fields he could see sunset flights of pigeons seeking their nests, black against the pink sky. The twin bell towers of the Marsaxlokk church felt so close he could reach out and touch them.

He had donated towards the building of that church, and had watched the progress of its construction. He had watched them hang the huge bells in the towers, a few years ago, but he had not been in that church for some time. Since he had approached one of the friars, to seek a blessing for the St Joseph shrine in the servants' courtyard.

He looked at the cigar between his fingers as if seeing it for the first time, then flung it down to the flagstones in the garden below, and watched its long death. The glowing end faded as tobacco scent rose to the height of where he stood, under the colonnade of his terrace. Would he have such a death; quiet, losing his glow, his energy, with no attention, ignored by all? Would no one come to his aid? Would he be crushed underfoot with a leather heel? Would he be consigned to the next world without a kind word or a single blessing? He often wondered how it would all end. Yet Marianna said they were only at the beginning.

Ah, Marianna. She was joyful now, joyful since her daughter lived, even though years had passed. She never took for granted a single day of her daughter's life – it was always 'the beginning' for her – and did not see how those poor young eyes were prisoners inside Prasseide's tortured face. How her once healthy body was ravaged by the disease that – despite all his warnings, all his careful concern – had come from the ports of the island to his house. To his very house. No one else was touched by it – not one of the servants, not a single peasant, not even Lazzaro. A wave of remorse clutched at his core. He was proud, arrogant. His hubris coned over his house like a miasma. He was punished for his conceit.

And yet his wife and daughter were happy. He called her his wife, but the friar at the church had informed him, in hushed tones, that she was not; that his hasty wedding in Naples could not be sanctioned in Malta. 'Unless you produce a certificate, Doctor – a Catholic certificate – one that we can recognize, because a hasty civil certificate, with two unknown witnesses, without church banns, cannot be ... it's not respectable, you see. It's not legitimate.' The friar's hissed whisper echoed on the church façade, underneath that half-monocle which would soon be filled with a mosaic which would cost so much money. Money the doctor had donated.

'You see,' the priest continued, as he fiddled with the rope at the waist of his black and white tunic, 'since you do not live in a sanctioned union, we cannot ...' His voice rose. 'Your house will have to be missed, passed over, during the *Tberik*, and that would be a great humiliation.'

The *Tberik* was apparently a serious consideration, even though it was a custom, a matter of heritage and habit, rather than a Church tenet or, as the friar would term it, a *precept*. It consisted of a priest and an altar boy visiting all the houses in the parish, door to door, bearing a silver pail of holy water and an aspergillum. There was also an incense burner. They would enter each residence, whose front doors – both the glass, and the substantial wooden ones – were thrown open, and stand in the hallway, which would be decorated appropriately. The incense burner would be swung a few times, and holy water sprinkled abundantly every which way, leaving a holy trail behind them. The occupants would stand in their entry with eyes respectfully lowered, and would cross themselves as they and their house were blessed for one more year.

It was almost two decades since this ritual was played out at Villa Sans Souci. Their double doors stayed closed for the entire day of blessing, and if anyone noticed along that desolate road, where the passage of carriages and carts and drays passed in their usual way, no one said anything. The doctor's family was more or less solitary. Sometimes, family members made the trip from Valletta. Very occasionally, Marianna entertained some community women in the gazebo of the garden, offering *biskuttini,* and tea from an enormous English silver teapot.

None of those ladies ever whispered a word of reluctance to attend the simple matinees, but if asked, the doctor doubted they would like to enter the main house of a couple not 'properly married'. He was sure word had got around about how they married in Naples. How she was an actress. How their haste was the result of passion, rather than sane, considered convention.

He had noticed that at the Valletta club where he sometimes showed his face, and at the hospitals and university, where he lectured and gave papers, ran surgeries and performed operations, he was listed as 'single and never married'.

He did not argue or try to change this. It was not as offensive as one might have thought. A number of island noblemen experienced the same treatment when they came off a ferry or a private schooner in the company of some foreign wife.

There was such a nobleman across the fields at Villa Marnisi, but he had taken the time to put his wife in a *karrozzin,* with its single well-groomed horse, bedecked with a wide satin ribbon the colour of ivory, and patient coachman, and hurry her off to some chapel on the way to Rabat, after posting banns in the correct way; and return home a perfectly valid married couple, in the eyes of the Catholic church.

'All it took was six weeks and a visit to a chapel, with Carmelina in a new hat, Luigi.' The baron spread his hands, rolled his eyes, and offered the doctor a cigarillo.

'It also took, Franco, a certain amount of compliance, acquiescence and ... what shall I call it? Submission.'

'Ha ha ha – you stubborn ass. I see you have not changed a bit. You will never change.'

Luigi laughed and nodded, and led the baron inside to a tray laden with a beautiful decanter of brandy and two glasses.

'Do you know what would be funny? If Marianna and I came to your villa and stood in line to be blessed at this year's *Tberik*. Ha ha.'

The baron nodded cheerfully. 'Carmelina would never allow it. She is more pious than the girls down at the fishing village.'

'But infinitely more elegant and circumspect with her language than a Marsaxlokk fishwife, eh?'

They laughed again.

Luigi thought of the ruddy healthy cheeks of the children of the fishing families. How healthy they looked, what rosy complexions they had, when they ran this way and that, bearing baskets of squirming fish to be sold door to door. How he wished his daughter looked like that. But she was neither that young nor that healthy.

Anxiety about her future, and what would befall her when he could no longer care for her was always on his mind. It was not going to be easy to discuss Prasseide's prospects with his wife.

After his brief interval with the baron, who took off on foot toward his own residence, the doctor entered the drawing room on the first floor. Marianna had done well in there, and the mirrors ordered from England, in their gilt frames, hung between the windows. He looked at his reflection repeated along the room; his greying head, bushy moustache, oval spectacles ... he looked good for his age. But he wished it was he who contracted smallpox rather than Prasseide. Ah Prasseide – how was she to make a life for herself? She was unmarriageable.

'There you are, Luigi!' Marianna, dressed for dinner, swept in. 'Will you not change your jacket?'

'Not tonight. I'll come down like this, if you will allow it.'

She smiled and looked at his tweed hunting jacket. 'You have been riding.'

'No – I knew the baron would not be um ... in the most superb suit, so I dressed accordingly.'

They laughed together. The Villa Marnisi residents might be noble and endowed with good looks, but they cared little about what they wore.

'Franco takes on a permanent country air, even in his dress.'

'Marianna – should we start to think of Prasseide's future? She is ... how old?'

His beautiful wife turned sad eyes to his own. 'We cannot discuss this at dinner. It is a subject I dare not raise with her. She's happy, Luigi. She embroiders, paints, and dreams of playing the harp. She knows you will buy her reams of new music to play. She is content.'

'But she has no friends. She has no future. Even if I endow her with a considerable fortune, who will have her?'

His wife's stern expression almost stopped the professor talking. 'I will not have her *married off!* As long as there is life in me I shall have her by my side.'

'Marianna ...'

'That is all I shall ever say.'

'*Marianna ...*'

'It's all I shall ever say. She will remain here with me, until my last breath is taken. Until yours is breathed. And the house will endure. She will be here until the last stone, the last slab, the last marble tile, the last plaster moulding is gone.' She said the words standing on the landing, in front of the beautiful mural. Her presaging words resounded on the marble stairs, the twin arches, the painted walls. Her finger pointed upward, to mark her words, it pointed, trembling, at the *tromp l'oeil* mural behind her, and her eyes blazed.

'Marianna ...'

'Mark my words, Luigi – our daughter will be here until the last of this house is *dust*.'

*

Five

Strip of gravel

The doctor returned to the house, parked the rental tightly against the rubble wall on the narrow asymmetrical strip of gravel that separated the property from the road, turned off the engine and sat back. Seven days, and he had not touched that expensive ladder. Seven days, and two dismal phone calls back home to Melbourne held him in a kind of limbo. Dismal, dismal. No hope in anything he could hear from Meg's end. She was sick of what she called his distractedness. Sick of him, in short.

'I say things about myself, and you seem totally shocked and unaware of anything that's to do with me. I've changed, Philip. Being a wife and a mother has changed me, but you haven't noticed. Twenty-five years, and you haven't noticed a *thing*.'

She was right. Of course she was right. But he had spent twenty-five years working like a demon, setting a small new practice on its way to undeniable success, treating patients with more than just medicines; pouring his whole being into terminal diseases, viruses, epidemics ... and perhaps that was where the whole reason of Meg's disappointment lay. He poured his whole being into medicine, and little or nothing into his home life. He left it to her.

'And now there you are, off to the other side of the globe, to push an old obsession into action. What about *us*?' She ended all she said with emphasis.

What about them? Meg and the children seemed fine. They had everything they needed and more. She had her community projects; the youngsters would soon find careers of their own. University was expensive, but he had more than enough to put them through any courses they wanted. He had listened, wordless, sentence-less, listening to her well-formed phrases coming through on his phone. It was obvious she had mentally rehearsed this diatribe, so he let her speak. The decision he made was rash, reckless, but it pacified her. It made her stop and listen.

'I'll speak to the clinic tonight, Meg. I'll get the other doctors, I'll get Xander and Sarah and Sian-Mi to carry on without me for a while.'

'What?'

'I'll rent a place and stay here. Look – I'll stay here ...' He formed a plan as he spoke. 'I'll stay and ... and give us a few months apart. We need time apart, perhaps.'

Meg did not refuse.

'Don't call it a separation. I'm not thinking of it like that, Meg. I just ...'

'You just want time to spend in that damned *house.*' She was not wrong.

Philip did not contradict her. 'Whatever reason will ... it might make everything better.' That's what he wanted above anything else; to make things better.

She relented. 'It might.' She did not ask how long he intended to stay in Malta.

Philip ended the call with a steady thumb, his head full of different thoughts clamouring for precedence. The house won out, easily. Easily, all the research he had done, in any spare time he had, over the years that went between then and now, came to the fore. He had read about the wealthy doctor who had the house built, and had found a sketchy history of the property, and of the two towns from which it was equidistant.

'Marsaxlokk and Żejtun.' He stared at the windscreen of the rental, knowing he should not be there; that he should be somewhere else, seeking accommodation. He had a three-month visa, but he wanted to stay longer. Someone said all he had to do was take a ferry to Sicily and return, to get a further three months, but he had no idea whether that would work. Sicily was barely 200 kilometres away. Would it work, or was it better to visit the Australian High Commission to stretch his stay?

The doctor raked a hand through greying hair. He raised his chin and looked at the car roof, then closed his eyes. The high-pitched ring of a carriage bell quickly made him blink and open them again. It was dark, unexpectedly quite dark, except for the glow from a yellow aura around a street lantern a few yards away.

He was standing in the way of a one-horse carriage, with the wind in his hair, and the coachman was getting impatient.

'Ser tiċċaqlaq, sinjur?'

The man spoke Maltese, but there was no mistaking what he meant. Philip was asked, in an assertive yet gentle tone, whether he was going to move.

He felt the horse's breath, exerted after a long drive. He felt a strong breeze; sea air from behind him. He took a number of steps backward and watched the coachman turn carefully, ring the bell twice, and guide the horse to a side gate, where a woman, whose head was swaddled in a white kerchief, undid the latch and let the carriage through.

Through bleary eyes, the doctor watched as a man alighted from behind a leather curtain on the carriage. He muttered a salutation and stood for a moment under the portico of the house while the horse clopped away to be unyoked and settled for the night. The front door opened, and the man entered the ornate hallway, which was just visible from the road.

Possessed by insatiable curiosity, Philip followed the carriage and slipped in through the gate just as the servant closed it. He watched the horse drink deeply from a metal bucket. He watched as the coachman took off his jacket, rolled up his sleeves, pushed a broom to one side, unhooked a lantern from a nail on the wall, and walked out onto the cobbles.

'Għadek hawn?'

Philip nodded. How was it possible that he understand this man? 'Yes, I'm still here.' He answered in the same language, a guttural yet smooth tongue as complicated and dense as it was beautiful to the ear. 'I'm still here. *Għadni hawn.*'

'Do you want me to show you the field, then?'

'The field?'

'Aren't you here to see the land?'

Philip was startled, but nodded. 'The land ... yes, yes, show me the land.'

'Before we do that, I must eat. I have just returned from Valletta. Do you know how long it takes to *ċeklem-ċeklem* all the way from Valletta?'

Philip had no idea, but he followed the man through a small courtyard. He noted the neatness of the place, the plants in terracotta pots, the shrine to some saint in a well-ordered niche in the corner.

'Saint Joseph.'

Philip nodded.

'Just a nod? Cross yourself. You foreigners are all the same.'

The candid scolding surprised Philip into silence.

But the man stood back and held out a hospitable arm. 'My wife always cooks enough for twice the number of souls in our family. You are most welcome to join us. I don't know what she has prepared, but can you smell that? I'm hungry. Go inside.'

A woman and two youths sat at a small table in a neat kitchen, where a stone hearth belched low flames. Over it, in a brown earthenware pot, something fragrant simmered gently.

'See? There is always something good on the *fuklar* in our kitchen, thank God.'

In silence, Philip sat on a stool to which he was motioned by one of the youths. They all bent their heads and crossed themselves, before the woman ladled a thick red cauliflower stew into unmatched bowls. They all took bent tin spoons from the middle of the table, where Philip saw a saucer full of glimmering sea-salt crystals. There was no wine. There was only water drawn straight into thick glass tumblers from a rudimentary tap over a tin trough.

'See? We have running water inside the house.'

Philip saw their perception of luxury, and was awed by it.

'You are here to see the land.' One of the youths, who had a bad squint and an uneven beard, looked at him over the bowl he held under his chin. He ate cauliflower in its thick tomato sauce, pushing dribbles back into his mouth with the back of his hand.

The meal had a dreamlike quality. Philip could not taste the stew, could not sense saltiness, even though he felt rough crystals between his fingers when he sprinkled salt over his steaming bowl. His tongue felt too large for his mouth. His eyes were grainy. 'How can we see the land at night?'

They looked at each other and back at Philip, and laughed. They looked at him staring down into a bowl which was empty. His eyes seemed mystified and dull, as if he had no notion of where he sat, and with whom.

'Are you not from the south? Are you North Italian?'

He did not know what they meant.

'It's summer. It's a clear night. There will be a moon in a while. Clear as day. You'll see.'

He saw. They all went out into the courtyard, where a big round moon, yellow as butter, round as a coin, made its appearance over the top of a distant carob tree.

'*Qamar kwinta.*' They spoke of the full moon as if it belonged to them, and not to the entire population of Earth's creatures. It was theirs alone. These people lived by the seasons, by the weather, by the signals and signs dealt to them by their climate and the passage of astral bodies through their sky. Their sky.

'Come, let's do it before the moon turns red – we'll go through the little gate, across the garden of the house, and then through the big gate to the fields. It will show us the way, better than any lantern.'

They were right – it was all clearly visible before him. Philip felt the chill, which he felt existed only for him. In their shirtsleeves, the two brothers seemed comfortable. The coachman had stripped to a navy-style woollen sleeveless singlet and old pinstripe trousers that someone had patched on the seat more than just once. Old leather braces looped on either side of him, swinging against his thighs. He had not abandoned his cloth cap the entire evening.

The house garden was a magical place. Once through the small gate, they stood still for a moment.

'Agħlaq ix-xatba warajk.'

Philip heard. He was being treated like one of the sons, rather than a privileged visitor, after all. Being told to close the gate behind him, he did what he was told.

There, exposed to his night eyes, the white-flowered garden of the villa spread before him. 'Only white flowers,' he said to himself.

'Heh, heh! I heard you. And blue, and blue! But the blue ones disappear at dusk, and all you can see are the white flowers, in the dark, and smell their scent, too. The jasmine is ...' He sniffed audibly.

Philip followed suit. In with the glorious night scent of jasmine was the eerie lingering smell of sandalwood. 'I smell something else.'

'Ah, yes. A little. And only in your head, eh? The memory of fine perfumes from the house, of the *sinjura*. She used to have fine things sent to her, by ship. But what you smell now is jasmine, only jasmine.'

By *sinjura* Philip understood *lady of the house*. He could picture in his head a woman's yellow skirts slithering up the staircase. Her hand replacing the crystal stopper in the neck of a sandalwood scent bottle. Yellow? *Yellow?* How on earth could he know that?

'Is she at home? Will she see us through the windows?'

The old man and his sons stopped. Moonlight shone on their turned faces, their eyes seemed darker than before. Karist scratched the grey hairs on his chest, which spilled over the neckline of his singlet, then scratched the back of his neck. 'Surely you know, sir, if you came to view the lands, that they are for sale for a reason.'

Philip looked up at the enormous moon, which was turning red, and over whose face thin cloud had started to scud. 'A reason?' He felt foolish.

'The lands would not be for sale unless ... look, surely you know. The poor *sinjura* has been dead now for ... how many years, Pawl?'

One of the youths laughed. 'How do you expect me to remember? I think I was still too young to go to *duttrina*. I didn't need doctrine class yet.'

His old father took a swipe at his son's head. 'Hey! Respect, please! We are never too old or too young to listen to the doctrine.' He turned to Philip. 'I think she died about fifteen years ago, sir.'

'So the daughter is alone.'

Karist exclaimed something profane. 'No, sir! When we say *sinjura* we mean the daughter. The parents passed away before her. I was a youngster when we all came to live here with my father, the first coachman. Do you know – the servants' house was built new, especially for the staff. Like at a palace. Heh, heh.'

'Oh.'

'Oh yes, indeed. Poor *sinjura* – you know I only ever saw her face ... ah, terrible. After her father died. And I shall never forget it. She was badly scarred by the smallpox, which she caught as a child.'

'Smallpox.'

'Yes – she um... she did not outlive her poor sick

father by much.' He nodded and did not seem to want to say more. 'How old could she have been? I don't know. In her twenties, perhaps.'

'So who ...?' Philip turned to look at the house.

'The cousins from Valletta descended upon the place at first. Heh heh.' There was no humour in his laugh. 'They did not stay very long.'

'Then?'

'Then a series of tenants. Few stayed longer than a year.'

'So if someone were to ...?'

The old man knew what he meant. 'Whoever buys the lands gets the house, sir. And the servants' quarters, and my services... with it.'

'But I just saw you bring a gentleman to the door.'

The old man was silent. His eyes were dark. He seemed to waver in the moonlight.

'But ...' He wanted to use his name. Karist; the man's name was Karist. 'Karist – who was it?'

The old man turned and started towards what he called the big gate. Their lives were ordered by a small geography; smaller than the tiny island on which they lived, bounded by the Small Gate and the Big Gate. By the road to Żejtun, the road to Marsaxlokk Bay, the road to Valletta. The clip-clop of the horse.

'Who are the gentlemen who come to the house, eh? Who knows? They have no names.'

What did he mean?

'Everyone has a name.'

The old man nodded. 'So what is yours, sir?

'I'm Doctor Philip Falzon, from Melbourne.'

They arrived at the big gate. To one side, Philip glimpsed a structure covered by jasmine creeper.

'A doctor? A doctor? Do I hear the truth, or are you ...?'

'What's that?' The doctor pointed at the structure.

'A fancy summerhouse ... we call it *il-gaziba.*' He shrugged. 'It hardly holds four chairs in comfort. The old people used to stand in it, and look out over the fields to Marsaxlokk.'

'Oh – can we?'

'Not if you fancy your nice straight bones. It's a ruin, and dangerous. The foundation stones were not żonqor, you see.'

'What's żonqor?'

The coachman unhooked the big gate and they went through. 'Dense limestone. It turns grey with time, after it's cut from the quarry. Soft stone is called *franka*, and hard stone is żonqor. I thought everyone knew this.'

Philip smiled and nodded. He knew now.

They turned to look at a sloping expanse of field, bound by rubble walls and clumps of prickly pear. There was another ruin here, an ancient rounded shape the doctor could plainly see in the moonlight. Its low roof had caved in, some time in the remote past, and its rounded walls made of random found rocks from the surrounding fields were crumbling.

'It cannot be used,' the old man said.

'That's obvious.'

'I mean – this *girna,* which is a shelter for hunting, cannot be used for the reason it was made, because these fields are no longer reserved.'

The doctor knew the man would go on and explain.

'Reserved for hunting. The permit has expired ... and it didn't exactly happen yesterday, you know.'

'Karist – I like these lands.'

'He heh. Four *tumoli,* or four *tomniet,* it says on paper. What is left ... I do not know how much is left, after, you know, farmers move their walls and fences. They pull prickly pear from their side, and it grows thicker on the other, further away from them. They axe a carob tree, and all of a sudden they have a *qasba* or two more.'

'*Tomniet? Qasba?*'

'Like that we measure land here. *Tomna, qasba* ... that's what we say.'

The moon was now directly above their heads. It cast eerie light over the brown stony soil, and threw stunted shadows of carob trees and the derelict hunting shelter. The coachman's shadow was thrown around him in a circular way, because of his rounded belly.

'Look – you have no shadow!' He pointed at the doctor's feet. 'He heh. You must be some sort of *babaw*. Heh heh.'

Dizziness, mind fog descended and the doctor felt unwell. He gulped for air. 'Bab...'

'*Babaw*. You are like a ghost, and your face is white enough. I do not believe in spirits, you know, although they say that the people who visit the house ... I should not tell you or you will never buy the land. No *babaw*. No ghosts, all right? Just ordinary human sadness. Oh, and happiness, of course.' He added that quickly, not to put Philip off. 'Do you have enough money?'

'What's the asking price?' Unsteady on his legs, the doctor followed Karist through the big gate, then the little gate, where the overpowering scent from the house, of sandalwood, of incense, of something ethereal and unnameable, assaulted his breath. 'I must sit down for a while.'

'*Qisek rajt xi ħares.*'

'What?'

'You look like you've seen a ghost.' The old man coughed. 'Not surprising, around these parts, but I don't believe. Would I still be here if I believed in ghosts, eh?'

They reached the latched gate to the road.

'Are you all right? You're still very pale.'

'Yes ... yes. I have kept you long enough.'

'Goodnight, then. Come again when you have enough money, heh heh!' The old man shuffled away

49

towards his small house next door to the villa.

Philip took two more steps. It was all that was possible; he slid his back down against the wall below the railings and slithered to the ground, breathing deeply. The moon was now out of sight.

The doctor raised his head, closed his eyes tightly, and opened them again, feeling queasy. The steering wheel nearly touched his thighs. The mobile phone was dead in his hand, the sky was pink with the sun's early rays, and the clock on the dashboard read *5:23 am*.

*

Six

Bare stone

From the space at the bottom of the stairs, stairs which were no longer there, the doctor looked upward. He craned his neck to try to determine the state of the mural on the landing.

It was still there. It was not too streaked with mould or rainwater runnels. Some miracle protected it, even in the last twenty-five years, during which he had thought of it every single day. It was some kind of exceptional miracle, exceptional good fortune, because the rest of the house was close to complete dereliction. 'This place ought to be condemned. I'm lucky there's no notice outside forbidding trespass.' He spoke to himself, wondering how he was to get up on the fragile landing to have a closer look. 'It's about time I brought that ladder in.'

It was not easy. Even though manufactured from aluminium, in what the label said was a 'light, and easily portable design' the ladder was obviously made for two men to carry and unfold. It was the kind that could be bent into various configurations; a scaffold, a bench, a stepladder, telescopic steps, electrician's or house decorator's platform. How far did it reach as a simple ladder? There was nothing simple about its design, despite the illustration on the label. *Easily converts to four positions. Full extent, 19 feet.*

He finally managed to wrest it to its longest single stretch, and with some difficulty, positioned its top against the only level place up on the jagged extremity of the ruined landing, where once a beautiful banister graced the edge, and where now the blunt brown ends of old metal beams protruded. It did not bend in the middle under his weight as he feared it might. The doctor climbed, climbed and hoped he could secure it in some way to the top, because if it toppled away sideways, he was doomed to spend a long time on that landing with no way to get himself down again.

Unsure footing, and a very fragile platform to stand on. The stone slabs did not quite fit between the beams. At any moment, he expected one or two to crash to the floor below. Hopefully, not the one he stood on to survey the effect of time on the mural.

It survived. Vandalized, spattered with daubs of vermilion paint, bearing the marks of trespassers through the years, displaying their scrawls, gouges and graffiti, it was still there. A view of the landscape to the west of the house, through a bower laden with blue and white wisteria. Were those purple grapes, a vine? It was difficult to decide. Someone had scrawled and scratched METALLICA across a dense area of dark green foliage. Someone else had inscribed initials and a matchstick hangman.

And there was a face. A well-enough executed youthful face, done in more colour than one would have on hand without pre-deliberation. Who had painted that face among the blue and white flowers? It was obviously not in the original style, done much later. Decades later. Was it the face he saw that first time? He did not think so.

'Hey! Hey – who's up there? Are you mad? It's dangerous.' A male voice, from below, thundered and resounded on the limestone block walls. 'Hey, can you hear me?'

Philip Falzon approached the spot where his ladder rested against the edge and looked down upon the foreshortened shape of an older man in shorts and t-shirt. Large sunglasses covered most of his face.

'You came equipped for a good look, I see.'

Philip did not reply. He looked downward, wondering what to say, buying time by clearing his throat and taking two deep breaths.

'Hello? Did you hear me? *Smajtni?*' He tried a handful of languages, including Maltese.

'I heard.' Philip took one step more, afraid to venture too close to the edge. 'Don't touch the ladder.'

'Ah. Are you English? Interested in old places, eh? There are lots more, and lots better than this one.' The man took hold of the ladder and placed a foot on the first rung.

'No! Stay there. Don't come up. This landing can't take us both. It's fragile. It will crash – it will collapse.' Philip exhaled slowly. He guessed the man wanted to speak to him without having to crane his neck. 'Look – I'll come down.' He turned, placed his feet carefully, one after the other, in the right places, and sensed the stranger was holding the ladder as he descended.

'You could have used the *garigor*.' He whipped off his sunglasses the moment they stood face to face. 'I'm Tony. I live across the road, a bit that way, towards the sea. I've seen your car before.'

'Oh?'

'Interested in the place? It's been for sale for years. No one wants it. And now, now that it's vandalized and condemned ...'

'I saw no notice. There are no signs to say it's dangerous.'

He smiled, folded the glasses, and put them in a breast pocket very carefully. 'Things that are plain don't have to be written down on a notice.' He winked. 'In any case, it's also plain you haven't found the *garigor*.'

'I don't know what that is.'

'Obviously.' Tony shrugged and smiled. His expression suggested that anyone in his right mind would have sought a *garigor*, whatever it was. 'Follow me. Not many people have discovered it. This place is mainly visited by young people, daring each other to stay the night and meet the ghost.'

Philip guessed Tony would rattle on and tell him what he knew without having to be prodded or prompted.

'Now – *ħares* or *fatat* ... that is the question.' Tony exploded in a massive laugh, which would have rattled windowpanes if there were any.

'Look, I don't understand.'

'I know. Of course I know.' Tony steadied himself by placing a hand on a door jamb of bare stone. Its architrave had vanished long ago. 'This place is haunted. Until just after the war, it was still occupied. There was an English couple – tenants, I think. They ran a boarding house. It didn't have a good reputation. Perhaps the ghost was to blame. Or it was because the woman was a bad cook, by Maltese standards, or because of the vermin.'

'Vermin?'

'Cockroaches, mice ... farmhouses are usually beset by small mice because of stored grains.'

'But this wasn't a farmhouse.'

Tony nodded. Approval lit up his broad face and bright eyes. He moved towards the back of the house. 'Ah, so you know. Quite right, it wasn't. Neither was it some kind of summer house. It was lived in year-round, in its heyday. And just like the other villa, over the fields ... have you seen it? It's been done up. Just like that one, it has seen glorious days. Chandeliers, Persian rugs – you know, the lot. Luxury, you might say.' He clambered over a pile of broken stone blocks. 'See? Through here there is a walled-up doorway, so low few people see it.'

'And ...'

'And we can remove some of the stones ... like this.' He grunted and lifted a few sizeable pieces of masonry. With the side of his hand, using his whole forearm as a kind of broom, he swept and dusted away smaller fragments, and when the makeshift walling reached the height of his knee, he gave it a good kick. It fell inward with a rumble. 'After you.' He gave another deep laugh.

Philip found himself in a small dark space that smelled of stone dust and old human and dog faeces.

'Phew.'

'Ah – people are pigs. If you can ignore that for a minute, and look to your left, you will see the bottom of a stone winding staircase. What we call a *garigor*. It was used by servants, mostly, to access all storeys from the kitchen area ... which is where we are standing. The kitchen goes to there, roughly, where that pile is. That's what used to be the end of the kitchen. And those winding steps are the back stairs.'

Philip approached the small steps, all carved out of limestone, with a central hand-rest that wound upward. It was so narrow, and wound so tightly, it resembled the inside of a seashell. He said so to Tony.

'Ah – we are islanders. Perhaps that's where our ancestors got the idea.' His eyes twinkled. 'Are you brave enough to go up? Go on, climb a few of those steps.'

'First explain what you said before, Tony. About ghosts.'

'Climb. Climb to the first landing, to get out of this smell.'

'High enough?' Philip came to a tiny unglazed window, and a narrow landing, which was really one large triangular step. Just over it, in the wall, was an alcove built into the thickness of the wall.

'That's called a *gabinett*. Used by servants for folded bed linen, towels, rolled rugs ... you know. Shall we go higher?'

'Um ... no. I ...'

'Ha ha! She won't be waiting at the top, you know! Ha ha ha! These are servants' places. She'd be out front, walking on that landing where you so carefully placed your brand new ladder. It must have cost you a pretty penny.'

'She? *She?*'

Tony shook his head and finger in the same way and at the same tempo. 'Don't tell me you are here to see rubble and debris. What's your name, anyway?'

'Philip.'

'Philip – I know you've heard things in the fishing village.'

'Well ...'

'Wherever. The White Lady is a well-known haunting.'

Philip waited. The man mentioned two strange words before they got to the winding staircase. If he kept silent, Tony might mention them again.

'People see a woman in a white dress, with a veil over her face. Some people say she's in black. Some have seen her at the windows, or on the terrace when the moon is full.'

'The terrace has collapsed.'

'Ghosts don't need slabs to walk on, Philip. Some have seen the hallway lit up at night. It's a *ħares*, or a *fatat*.'

'All right.' The words confused him. 'What are those?'

'Do you only have one name for ghost in English?'

Philip scratched the back of his neck. 'Um... no. Apparition, spirit, presence, phantom, wraith ... um ... spook, illusion, spectre. I think there are more.'

'Very good. Good words. You are good with words! Which one means a ghost that takes care of something? Like ... protects a building or a family, or some sort of treasure?'

'Oh,' Philip shrugged. 'I don't think ...'

Tony laughed. He took a step back and sat on a narrow stone step. With a hand on each knee, he continued. '*Ħares* is that kind of ghost. A spirit, a presence – see, I can use your words – that guards something. From a word that means to protect. *Ħares*.'

That was interesting.

'And *fatat* is the opposite. It's a spooky ghost that scares the life out of people in a house because it wants them to go away, or wants to punish them for something. They usually live on staircases.'

'What? *Live?*'

'You know what I mean.' Tony shifted, uncomfortable with the explanation of a malevolent ghost. 'They haunt stairways, and do all sorts of negative and destructive things. Including frightening people.'

'A vengeful kind of ghost.'

'So one ghost can be vengeful, as you put it. And another might be benevolent.'

'Benevolent?'

'Benign – not harmful.'

Tony beamed. 'Oh – but the same ghost can be both things. Nice to some, and horrible to others.'

This was becoming complicated. 'What ... a *ħares* and *fatat* rolled into one?'

He did not get the humour. 'Well, some people call it one thing, and others call it the other, depending on how it treats them or makes them feel.' Tony laughed out loud. 'So how do you feel right now? Do you want to climb more steps?' His tentative laugh was flattened as he approached the next section of the carved winding structure. 'She won't be at the top, I tell you. Ha ha ha.'

'So you remember the English couple and their guest house?'

Tony was out of breath ahead of Philip. He heard him groan as he climbed. 'No. I'm from Għaxaq. I've only lived here since I married my Helen. Her people remember all sorts of things. They say it was a brothel at one time, and vacant for long periods ... and then for brief periods occupied by people who packed all their things into a van in a hurry, and were never seen again.'

'Spooked.'

The man up the steps, out of sight but audible, trumpeted a huge laugh in the small space. 'Ha ha ha! Spooked! Ha ha. *Spooked.*' He laughed and laughed, and Philip met him, sitting down at another of those landings where a tiny room led off a corner triangular step.

'See how thick the walls are? But not as thick as some of those medieval places in Mdina and Rabat. This place was only built in the mid-eighteen hundreds. Same time, more or less, as the laying of the foundations of the Marsaxlokk church. You know – Our Lady of Pompeii.'

'I must go down to the bay and visit it.'

'People say it was built in a year. But nothing in Malta is built in a year. Hahaha! Ha Ha! Not anything the size of that church, with two bell towers and a dome. Mind you, I think the dome came much later. The bay was bombed in the war, you know.'

The third landing opened out into a narrow passage between ruined rooms with perilous floors. Philip looked down three storeys through gaping holes. But people had come this way before them, perhaps not as many as on the floors below. Graffiti, gouges, spatters of paint and goodness knew what other liquids adorned the walls. The roofs of the rooms were caved in, so what remained aloft, and the loose flooring underfoot, looked so precarious Philip did not want to venture in. But a shiver, a sensation of what was once an atmosphere of wealth and abundance, elegance and good fortune shifted the hairs on the back of his neck. 'Ah. I do envy people in those days. Life was so much more graceful and sedate.'

Tony did not agree. 'Well, Philip – it depended a lot on their class, and whether they knew their place and were happy in it. It's easy to enjoy life when money is no object. But think of servants running up and down these narrow winding back steps with hot water, clean shirts, polished shoes, dirty boots. Up and down, up and down, three storeys high, all day. What else did they carry up and down? I don't know.'

'Candles, lamps? Vases of flowers? Look – I expect so, Tony. But life now is so frenetic, I kind of suffer from nostalgia.'

'You can be nostalgic for something you never experienced? Only movie-makers can do that!' He laughed again. 'But yes, even I sometimes think how it might have been if I had a horse and cart rather than my van, whose exhaust manifold needs replacing.'

Philip did not know why, but he thought of long mirrors in gilt frames, and a beautiful *tromp l'oeil* trellis on the side of a wide curving staircase. He thought of a room with a coved ceiling, walls covered in damask, and a splendid harp standing near a small gilt chair. Had he seen such a room? Had he seen such an instrument?

They left the building together, with Tony carrying the folded ladder effortlessly. He slid it easily into Philip's rental car. 'Don't forget. If you're down this way again, knock on the third door down there ... see?' He pointed. 'The only dark red front door in the row of houses on the left. And we'll have another chat. Goodbye!'

*

Seven

Winding staircase

The thin man sat on the gazebo steps in the garden. It would soon be dark. Gradually, all that could be seen would be white flowers. But his face was in his hands. He could see nothing. Even if he allowed his tear-filled eyes to gaze over the beds in front of him, he would see nothing. Grief, remorse, and dread gripped him, and he could think of nothing else.

He listened to his own laboured breathing with a kind of disgust. Nothing, nothing had gone right since he accepted this commission. He should have let the professor employ some other artist. Some other fool willing to come all this way to the nether parts of the island, where everything was doomed, cursed. Lost. He was lost. The kingdom of heaven would be closed to him, and he was destined to writhe in despair for eternity.

'Oh. Oh. Oh ... oh. What am I to do? What have I *done*?'

There was a high pitched sound somewhere to his left.

'*X'ser nagħmel, pipistrell?*' Oh, he was reduced to talking to a tiny bat, which flew instinctually, without having to see where it went, or whence it came. He looked up, and in the last light of the day, saw the bat enter one of the unglazed windows of the narrow winding staircase, which was alive with servants during the day, and a small haven for tiny bats at night. They were cathedral bats. Church bats. He *knew* whence they came. The bell towers at the bay in Marsaxlokk were full of them, someone said.

He knew the cathedral belfries in Mdina housed many bats. The artist Turu Manche, who had restored a painting there, told him how he had casually inserted his hand into the mouth of a dormant cannon, one of a pair of acting decorative sentinels on the Mdina cathedral forecourt, and unwittingly touched the slick back of a bat. It flew out into his face, and he swore never to touch a cannon again.

'There are dozens of bats in hell. They will fly in my face for eternity. I will gnash my teeth in disgust and fear. And it will serve me right.'

'What are you saying, Lazzaro? What madness is this?'

'You should have taken on Calì's son. Anyone would have been better than me to paint your mural.'

The doctor drew closer. His cigar end glowed in the dark. 'What's done is done. We cannot undo it now. Nobody can. It was not really your fault. This is just fate pushing us all before it.'

Lazzaro placed his face in his hands one more. 'But your poor daughter, Luigi – her countenance is withered forever. I saw her properly for the first time, this afternoon. She usually peeps from behind the drawing room door. She watches us. Always from a distance, from beneath the peak of her bonnet. Today I saw her face ... It's ... it's ... Her entire life is without expectation. You'll never find her a husband.'

Luigi hitched his trousers from the creases and sat next to the artist.

'You'll ruin the seat of your trousers.'

'Do you think I care about my trousers? Do you want a cigar?'

'No, thank you.'

The two men sat in silence for a few minutes.

'Luigi, listen. My painting career is over anyway. I can bestow an income on her, to take her into her future without need to seek a husband. What do you think of that?'

'Hush. Hush, Lazzaro, for heaven's sake. For the sake of God in heaven. Your career is not over. You will go on to paint the inside of many church domes.'

'Perhaps I can make amends that way.'

'You will paint many madonnas.' Luigi looked

up at the louring sky. 'And Prasseide will be all right. I will provide her with enough. You have daughters of your own. Do not let Marianna hear you say such things. She will not listen to a word about money, or husbands, or the future, or fate ... or anything, when it comes to Prasseide. Sometimes I think she cannot see our daughter's ravaged face. She has time for you, which is surprising – she has stopped blaming you. Even I blamed you at first.' The doctor placed his face in his hands, with the cigar still glowing between his fingers.

Bats flew overhead. They made a strange sound that was just audible in the still air. 'Bats.'

'Bats.'

'She lived, Lazzaro. We must be grateful that she survived. Children in Marsa and Valletta died.'

The thin man did not say what he thought. He did not say she might have been more fortunate to die. 'Have you thought of a convent? The nuns would ...'

'Hush! If Marianna hears you she will never allow me to forget it. She is overjoyed that Prasseide has survived. She is trying to decide between a piano and a harp for her.'

'What?'

'We are sending to Rome for a nice harp.'

The artist shook his head. 'You are such strong and determined people ... not defeated by anything. How is that? How do you assume such confidence? I envy you that, if nothing else. Your daughter's face, her entire body ... her ... and you think of buying a harp!'

'And the maestro from Żejtun will come and instruct her. It will take the place of my reading and writing lessons with her. Every Thursday afternoon. And it's Marianna who is strong. Not I.'

Lazzaro shook his head in wonder. He looked up at the house. It was lonely out there on the road to the bay at Marsaxlokk. He had lived there for months on end, and could not wait to get back to his home town, Senglea.

'The harp will cost a great deal of money. And some say it is not seemly for a woman to play such an instrument, but I have seen performances in Italy, and I admire the talent of such musical ladies.'

'It is hardly decorous ...'

'For charity. At charity concerts. It is fine. Things are changing, Lazzaro. In Europe now, being on the stage is almost lauded. And you think I say these things because of Marianna. She was an actress, true, but look at her – there are not many ladies ...'

'You're right. Absolutely right. None more elegant or so refined. A proper lady. And such fortitude and strength. Such resilience in the face of adversity.'

'And do you see how much love she pours into everything? I'm so blessed in that way. Prasseide is so fortunate in that regard.' The doctor raised his head so that his eyes would not fill with tears and spill over. 'Ah! My daughter. My daughter.'

'Luigi, do you believe in...'

'Hush, Lazzaro. I believe in nothing. Perhaps that's why this damned thing has happened. I believe in nothing, do you hear? Perhaps this is a punishment, because I rarely go to church. Because the priest passes this house over during the *Tberik*.' He sighed.

'Really?' The artist sounded appalled.

'Yes. We keep the doors closed and he marches right past with his altar boy behind him. People come and watch the whole thing, the whole stupid puerile thing – it is humiliating. It might also be because I never planned for a chapel to be built, when this house was designed. My cousins in Valletta were scandalized, and ... but the new church at Marsaxlokk is so close, I said to them. As if I would be some sort of regular worshipper there. But I sent the Dominican monks money. Plenty of money. They have ordered a statue to be carved. Out of the finest wood, in Italy.'

'And I suppose you ...'

'Of course. I pacified Dun Salv with a promise that nothing would stand in the way, and he would get his statue. The Holy Mother and Child, and Saints Dominic and Catherine.'

'I thought it was the baroness, who survived that dreadful tempest, who gave money for all that.'

'She did – a number of us donated ... and donated generously. That church would never have been built without great amounts of *liri*.'

The two men nodded greying heads together.

'The mural is long finished, Luigi. I'm returning to Senglea after dinner tomorrow.'

The doctor nodded. 'You don't know how to leave, is that it?'

A small groan of assent emerged from the artist's throat. 'I was so tempted to take base red paint and a wide wall painter's brush, and cover it all with a thick coat of red. Red. So that nothing ... nothing ...'

The doctor stood and turned, just as a fresh breeze blew in from the bay, setting branches swishing in the night. 'Oh – I'm so glad you did not do that!'

'Well, it's not mine. Since you paid me, it is yours. The wall is yours. How can I destroy something that doesn't belong to me? No matter how miserable it makes me.'

They started toward the house, whose windows blazed with light from the many lamps Marianna always had lit at sunset. 'Lamps!' she would exclaim. 'Light the lamps!' They had an array of the most beautiful glass-shaded oil lamps to rival any collection in the big cities of Cospicua, Senglea, and Vittoriosa. Their windows glowed more warmly than any in Valletta. Here, in the middle of nowhere.

'What is that I hear?'

'Music?'

'It cannot be. Marianna is sitting with Prasseide. They are embroidering. And the harp is still on its way. The phonograph lid is closed.'

'You have a phonograph! Fancy that – always the most modern things in your house.'

'Electricity is coming, too – the house will be wired up and there will be lights at the turn of a switch.'

'Expensive?'

'Abominably so.'

'Never mind. So you don't regret I didn't erase your mural, Luigi – the mural that brought you such misfortune?'

'Oh ... that would have been a disaster indeed. Prasseide loves it. She does not attribute her miserable state to your mural at all. In fact, she rather feels it is the highlight of these dubious months. My daughter has said a number of times, that as long as the mural is in this house, she will never want to leave. It makes her ... it makes her whole, she says, although I do not know exactly what she means. If it makes her feel whole, it must be preserved for all time.'

'That is a relief.'

'Enough said, then. We shall all bid you farewell tomorrow.'

'Wait, Luigi, wait – I beg your indulgence.'

'What is it, my friend?'

'You call me your friend, but I have wreaked a disaster in this house – a blight on your family which can never be reversed. I have no means to try to right the wrong, but please, listen to me.'

'I'm listening.' The doctor took a deep breath and broke off a sprig of jasmine from the creeper growing over his head.

'If you can bear my presence three weeks longer ...'

'Three weeks!'

'Yes – I shall send an order to Valletta tomorrow, for a stretched canvas, and I shall make you something to treasure.'

'I will need to pay you.'

'Definitely not. This will be from my heart, Luigi. A work to make amends, so that you can call me your friend, and mean it.'

*

Eight

Walled-up doors

The doctor pushed the key into the ignition and started the small rental car. He looked forward to resting at his accommodation at Xgħajra, which was more than just good. He had asked for a long-term bed and breakfast arrangement and found it was a small apartment with everything he needed, and the cost was not extravagant. He wanted a long shower and a night of nothing but a bit of TV, and then at least nine hours of sleep. Exhaustion seemed to overpower him on this trip. Drained, dog-tired, he would stagger from shower to bed and hardly remember dropping off. Were his body and mind recovering from a hectic twenty-five-year stint of constant work? Was he wallowing in the relief of not having to fight with Meg?

At the apartment, after his drive through traffic that was slow and busy, even at that time of night, he threw open the balcony doors and stepped out to inhale the ozone and light spume blowing off the rough sea directly ahead of him. The view was tremendous; it energized him and settled his head and heart. He was not the sailing or swimming type, but loved being close to the sea shore. And he could not get much closer than this. His eyes took in the stretch of rocky coast, and a long look at the horizon detected a distant oil tanker, which seemed immobile. It would be gone in the morning. So would his fatigue.

The sound of waves crashing on black rocks, the heady scent of salty water, the knowledge of being in the centre of the Mediterranean, made him happier than he had been for a while.

Looking out at the horizon again, he noticed the moon, which had been full a few days ago. It had risen out of nowhere, a spooky asymmetrical disk. With it came the ethereal memory of a conversation he overheard, between two men in the garden at the Villa Sans Souci. Two men ruing the disfigurement of a young girl, and discussing a mural – the mural on the landing in that curved staircase – like it was some charm, some object with magical properties. Who the men were he could not remember; but he remembered his own dazed feeling as he listened to their mumbled inflected words. The soft guttural words of a private conversation in Maltese. How could he possibly understand any of it?

And there were small birds flying around in the dark, from a small building in the field beyond the garden, to the small windows of the house. There were several small unglazed windows in a long vertical line, the height of three storeys. He knew now, since his conversation and exploration with Tony, that they conveyed air to the tight winding staircase called *garigor*. The birds kept coming, settling on the tiny curved windowsills, and disappearing. He had watched them for what felt like an eternity, then he was engulfed by the scent of jasmine, and he had started his car. No. Not birds. They were possibly bats. *Pipistrelli*.

The doctor raided the fridge, promising himself a shopping spree the following day. Would he subsist on cheese, olives, and a couple of slices of sliced bread at the bottom of a plastic bag, or should he change his shirt and take his luck at some local restaurant? Nine was not that late.

It certainly was not late for the crowd that gathered at the small Birżebbuġa restaurant. Obviously a popular place, it was almost impossible to park anywhere along its front, and just as hard to get inside. From the depth of the long narrow restaurant, where the din of voices, and the clatter of crockery and cutlery was deafening, he saw someone wave.

He turned to see who the lucky people were whose friend had snapped up a table, but no one seemed to wave back. Philip pointed at his own chest and grimaced a wordless question. The woman nodded. She smiled, smiled and waved again.

'I'm Charl Emmaus.' Her gruff voice implied he should know who she was.

'Hello. I hope you waved at me, Charlotte.'

'*Charl*. Aren't you the man who's bought Villa Sans Souci?' She indicated a chair.

'No – isn't it still for sale?'

'Everyone's here for the fish – you must have the fish of the day, and the amazing salad. Just wait till it arrives. Would you ... of course you'll have white wine?'

Philip Falzon's tiredness dissipated. 'I haven't ...' The noise and this woman's directness were like two shots of adrenalin. Coupled with the smells of delicious food being trayed at head height by some very fast waiters, it was only a second before he could answer, but she saw his pause.

'People have seen you walk in with a ladder.' It was more an indication of how impossible it was to do anything in secret on this island than a scolding.

He laughed. 'I've walked in with a ladder – and let me tell you it was not an easy thing to do. And am I supposed to ... um, have we met?'

Charl Emmaus looked up from under a prominent brow and a face so well made-up Philip had to examine it. Eyebrows, lips, eyelids, all painted impeccably, and skin perfectly smooth and contoured. It was like stage paint. Faux beauty. He wondered what she might look like without it.

'Look, I've been trying to find you – all the local hotels don't seem ...'

'I'm staying in a small flat at ... *Shy*-something.' He could not pronounce the name. 'Your place names are devilish to say.'

She laughed, which lit up her shrewd eyes. 'Xgħajra. Okay – you might give me your mobile number because I can get you a price ... I mean ...' Her hurried words tumbled over each other. 'And here comes our dinner.'

'Was it just coincidence that you ...?' There was something distinctly funny about this woman and the way she orchestrated the whole serendipitous meeting. Something Philip could not put a finger on.

'I'm in the area.' A mysterious and confusing answer.

Philip looked at the plate of fish he could not remember ordering. 'How ...?' He saw now that she had followed him, and had somehow entered ahead of him. 'You know this place well, then?' He was not about to let her take the upper hand.

When the waiter brought a wine bottle to the table, he saw it was already uncorked. He held up a hand. 'The wine list, please.' He watched Charl Emmaus out of the corner of his eye as she watched him. He held up an assertive hand for the waiter to see.

'Sir, all our wines are on the blackboard ...'

He looked toward the wall at which the waiter's finger wavered.

'One ... two ... four from the top. Chilled. And please uncork it here, at this table.'

Off the waiter went, grimacing and shaking his head. He must have the occasional client who would not be duped. Philip smiled. The woman sitting across from him would need more guile than a waiter.

'Charl. That's right, is it? Charl?'

'I've been called worse, um...'

'Philip Falzon.'

'Falzon! A Maltese name. So you are ... Maltese?'

'Australian. Melbourne is full of Falzons. And Merciecas. And Spiteris.'

She tilted her head, making large earrings swing and glitter. 'Philip – I can get you a terrific price for ...'

He held up a hand. 'I'm quite happy with my accommodation *and* my car rental.' He looked at the fish, which looked delicious, and started on his dinner.

In another minute, she did too, and in a second the waiter was uncorking a bottle of white wine that beaded with condensation.

He could see she had calmed down, since her attempt at a sale had been defeated. She talked a bit about the area. 'Have you been inside any local churches? A couple of local *festas* are coming up soon.'

'I'll make it a point to do so. I've seen street decorations going up. Is that what they're for?'

'Yes. You're very interested in this district.'

He parried. 'So are you, it seems. Are you from around here?'

'My father was Eastern European. My mother lives in Sliema. But let's not go into family history. Let's talk about *the White Lady*.' Her voice lowered in volume on the last words. The register too was low.

'Which lady?'

'You know what I mean, I'm sure. She appears to unfortunate souls if they happen to be in that house after dark, Philip. That house. The house into which you took a long, expensive ladder.'

'I ...' He did not know what to say next. He neither wanted to lie, nor to talk about what he had seen and felt. It was none of her business. It was private. Besides, he had started to doubt whether any of it had happened.

'You like that place. It stands on a ... the land is sizeable.'

'It's a ruin. My look inside, with my long and expensive ladder, showed me it's a wreck. The land has lain fallow for decades. It would need trucks and trucks of topsoil to bring it anywhere near ... what's that word I'm looking for?'

'Arable.'

He pointed a finger and smiled. 'Bingo. But as you say, it's a pity. A real shame. It must have once been a fabulous place.'

'I've never seen it occupied. Never inhabited, in

my entire lifetime. It's always been like that. We drove past it on weekends, on the way to Marsaxlokk, when I was a kid, and it always looked exactly the same. Walled-up doors and windows on the ground floor, empty windows upstairs, through which you can see the sky. All the *tkaħħil* is gone.'

'The ...?'

'The rendering – plastering.'

'Yes – all that's left is bare stone and some traces of whitewash and paint on the inside. And the so-called White Lady. Did you ever see her?'

'We always drove back before dark. But my parents knew several people who did, Philip.'

'Did?'

'See her.' She dabbed at her lips in a stagy over-done way with the bright blue paper napkin and sat back. 'Some say it's the ghost of a wh... um, *woman*, killed in a brothel fight.'

'Oh yes?'

She tilted her head and looked at the wine bottle, and quickly poured herself another glass. 'Others say it's the ghost of an opera singer who was held in the villa against her will. They hear her sing at night.'

'Always in white?'

Her smile was lopsided and forced. 'Hm – you must have talked to the locals. You must have. Sometimes she's seen in black.'

'Veiled. Like a widow.'

She looked up. 'Yes.'

'You *have* seen her, Charl.'

'No.'

'And you know it's her aura that's white, not her ... what do you call it, gown, frock? What she's wearing – her dress. Not that, but her aura.'

Charl reached for her bag.

Philip held out a hand. 'I'll get this.'

'Of course not. I was the one to get the table.'

'Tell me about ...'

She looked up, her heavy brow wrinkled for a

second with an expression Philip could not decipher. Ah, that was it. She had got him. She managed to draw him in to talk about the ghost. She would soon draw him in to discuss a sale of something; a purchase of something. Some tour. Some cruise. He knew sales people had strategies. Anything, to snag a commission. 'Charl ... is it a *ħares* or a *fatat*, do you think?'

She laid a number of banknotes on top of the waiter's bill. Her face was expressionless, a mask. 'You *have* been talking to the locals.'

'Why have you followed me?'

'Look – I'll be at the house tomorrow. Tomorrow at ... at some time. Or the next day. We can talk some more. Right now, I must be in Sliema to look after my poor mother.'

Philip watched her walk awkwardly between tables, on extraordinarily high heels. She seemed to have no waist; a straight up-and-down figure, Meg would have called it.

Meg; he needed to call her, to at least have a small chat. Talk to the kids if they were home. Philip started to calculate the time difference in his head.

*

Nine

Door jamb

The man in the pink waistcoat hung his head, reluctant to look at his reflection in the mirror. Why did he come here? He had finished university last year, nineteen nineteen, and look at him now. This was a house of ill-repute, which housed women of light virtue.

One of them, tall, thin, beautiful in a vulgar way, stood right behind him. She wore something a lady would never wear in front of a gentleman. He had never even seen his mother in such a garment. It was a peignoir, of some sort of light foreign fabric, with designs embroidered by some fiendish machine. Red dragons, water lilies ... what was he doing here?

'You seem tired, Marc.'

How dare she address him by name? But was this not, after all, what he acquiesced to when he came out here in that motorcar from Żejtun with his friend Laurence?

'You can take off your waistcoat. Let me help you.'

'No! No! I can do it myself. Let me ...' At all costs he had to keep her hands off him. And he was not about to remove his waistcoat. He watched her move to a corner of the room where a small wine table held a tray.

She poured some kind of liqueur into two small stemmed glasses. He could smell it. It was sweet sherry. It was inconceivable that she should offer him sweet sherry at this time of night.

'Will you have a drink?' She held the glass to him, and smiled.

Tawdry. Vulgar. She was vulgar. She had no notion of what it meant to be elegant, and yet she tried this charade, this dissemblance.

He grimaced. 'Sweet sherry?'

'From Spain.'

'From Msieraħ, more likely.' They were still reeling from the deprivations of a long World War. How was it possible to have sherry from Spain?

'What?' She frowned, then smiled quickly, to veil her discomfort.

'Have you ever in your life been further away than ... than ... ' Fury robbed him of words. He was angry at himself, for placing his reputation in jeopardy; his soul in danger.

She looked at him in a suggestive manner.

He lowered his head and clasped hands. *'Domine non sum digno ...'*

Her jaw dropped. 'Are you praying?' Her hand was still outstretched with the glass. The sweet smell filled the room.

'And you would do well to join me, young lady.'

She was used to doing what she was told. *'Domine ...'*

'Stop! Stop! How dare you?'

The glass was placed on the tray; her hands were wiped on the sides of her garment, in a common kitchen gesture. 'Well, I think you must decide what it is you want.' Her impatience was starting to puncture what she was trained to do. She did not know how to entertain this kind of gentleman. Usually they came, saw what they wanted to see, did what they wanted to do, drank what they were offered, lit a cigar, and went off, to be replaced by others.

The door flew open.

The man inhaled sharply. He was caught standing there, in his pink waistcoat. But it was not humiliation or embarrassment that made his mouth fall open. *Another one.*

In the doorway a woman stood, all in white. She looked like a bride, with a thin veil thrown over her face. The room went gelid with cold, and a draught blew in with her.

The prostitute screamed.

The man was struck speechless. He watched as the woman in the peignoir hurried out of the door, showing her bare heels. She seemed to pass right through the woman in white, whose veil, whose long dress, were not even flurried by the passing of the frightened woman.

'Who are you? How can you just enter a room without knocking?'

'I own this house. May I inform you that this house and all its lands are mine. Mine!' She seemed out of breath. 'I have been up and down those stairs all evening. Are you a suitor? Did you come here under some inducement ... of money, or land, or position, or influence with a politician? To ask for my hand?'

'A suitor? *No.*' Mystified, he tried to see her features under the veil, but they were blurred by the embroidered muslin.

'If you are not a suitor, you might do well to put on your jacket and descend the stairs. Someone will see to your departure. Someone might call the coachman for you. How did you get here?'

'By motorcar, of course. This place is at the end of the earth.'

'How dare you? This is the main road that goes from Żejtun to Marsaxlokk. It is an important thoroughfare. It is the only way to get to this villa and the one at Marnisi.'

'Exactly. Even with a motorcar, in nineteen twenty, it takes hours to get here. It's miles off the beaten track.'

'Nothing is beaten here – least of all *tracks*. Kindly take heed of what I say, and leave immediately. Otherwise ...'

The man turned, grasped his limp jacket by the neck, and started to shrug himself into it.

'Leave!'

He made a move towards the door, but the white

skirts were in his way.

'Leave!' The woman, pale as a wraith, lifted a hand, on which gleamed the spark of a diamond ring. She raised her veil, and showed him her ravaged face. 'You wouldn't want to marry this! You can't bear to look at it.'

'Ah!' He inhaled again, this time in real fear. Her pocked skin was so transparent and rutted he could see the architrave behind her, right through it. It was cratered and ruined, and seemed to have no vestige of a skull underneath, and yet ... and yet, he saw yellowish uneven teeth, like gravestones.

'Argh.' This was too much.

Down the stairs, out through the hallway, the man fled. Two girls, embracing each other in what looked like apprehension not entirely new to them, waited just inside the black railings.

'You saw her, didn't you?'

'Of course I saw her. Goodness! Who is she?'

One of the girls held a hand to her mouth. 'The white lady.'

The man adjusted his jacket and looked backward into the entrance. He was not about to enter again to summon Laurence. And Laurence was the only one who could start the car, since the keys were in his pocket.

'That is our car.' He felt foolish. It was parked at the side of the road a bit further than the streetlight.

'Here comes the other gentleman.' One of the girls announced Laurence, as if remembering her manners just at the last minute, at a time of disquiet and emotion.

'Laurence! Did *you* see her?'

The man's smile was wide and cheery, and he was pocketing a leather wallet inside his jacket. 'See who? Are you ready to go, Marc?' Distracted. Distracted and jocular. Happy to the extreme, even a little inebriated.

To Marc's mind, a happy sinner. His friend was

not touched, either by fear or remorse, or the apprehension he felt after seeing what he now knew was an apparition of the most dreadful kind. The kind that could punish.

In the motorcar, he gave Laurence a stammered account of what happened. How the door flew open, how the door jamb was visible through the pocked face of the intruder.

'Ha ha! Too much bad *Spanish* sherry, Marc!'

'I didn't touch a drop. Sherry, at this time of night. Bah!'

Laurence twirled the steering wheel as they rounded the bend into Żejtun. 'Perhaps you should have, then.'

One thing was certain. Marc would never again go that far along the road to Marsaxlokk. 'Who do you think it was, Laurence?'

'Who who was, you gullible fool? Get a grip of yourself.'

'I saw her, I tell you. And so did the... the ... *girl.*'

'You saw a figment. People around these parts are always talking about the White Lady. It's what they think up, to keep ordinary people away from the place. So they can carry on their business, which is not strictly legit. We might live in racy times, we might dance the Charleston, but some things ... You have fallen hook, line, and everything else for their local tattle.'

'But I'd never heard of her.'

'Sure you hadn't. Now I'll get you home and you can have some of your mother's black market brandy. Would that make you feel better at this time of night?'

*

Ten

Gazebo

She was seventeen, and clever; talented. She moved around the house gracefully, like her mother. A dressmaker would come to the house and measure her figure for each season's new clothes. A grey serge suit with a fur collar. A cheerful carmine skirt to wear with practical white blouses. A well-lined jacket for when they took the *karrozzin* down to the shore in the winter. Light-coloured lawn and muslin blouses to wear on the mornings she read, wrote, or practised the harp. They received catalogues from England and copied the designs, and looked at illustrations in newspapers and journals.

'Look – the princesses are wearing shorter skirts!'

'And enormous hats, look!'

A box of feathers and felt from Naples was soon turned, by some magic, into two delightful hats by Natalina, the seamstress, who had a wooden hat block she would steam. And boots and shoes came to the house from Hamrun, in beautiful boxes, to be tried and selected. There were black satin shoes with buckles that went well with dark green and deep purple, the colours Prasseide loved best.

They were beautiful clothes, made with love. And the dressmaker was now used to the young girl's gaunt scarred face, her lacerated arms, the shocking disfiguration of her skin, with dried hollows where the pustules had burst and withered.

'These are dark colours for such a young girl,' Natalina would say to the mother, who stood by while the young girl chose from swatches.

'It matters little.' The whispering did not reach Prasseide's ears. She wandered to the windows often, to look down into the garden. 'We should let her have the fabrics she wants. I like to make her happy.'

'I'll show her the pastel shades, and some new patterned cottons.'

'See what happens.'

Prasseide eventually chose a length of gorgeous striped linen in rainbow shades, for a blouse with pin-tucks down the front, but she only wore it rarely.

The disease had struck her vocal chords, which meant she was occasionally hoarse, and could certainly never sing. 'Sing, Mama – I love to hear you sing, because I can't.'

And Marianna would sit at the upright piano in the small front sitting room and tinkle out a happy tune, accompaniment to her singing. It was nothing like her acting, of course, which theatre critics on the continent had lauded with praise.

When she was younger, they had tried to renew contact with old friends, but the visits were awkward, the young people appalled, shocked by Prasseide's appearance. The parents kept up a semblance of politeness while they were there, and numbly drank tea and pretended to nibble at small cakes, but no one returned their invitations. No one came near their home again.

In the space of two years, they were solitary and isolated. Even more solitary than the doctor had intended when he had the house built.

He had taken to walking out on his own after sunset, ambling down the deserted road to the bay at Marsaxlokk. He would stand underneath a lamppost near the church on the square and smoke a cigar. Then he would wander to the water's edge, spend some time looking at starlight tremble on the waves, kick at a shell or a piece of flotsam, note the slow progress made on the new jetty, and return home slowly, his hair mussed by the sea breeze.

'Did you enjoy your walk, Luigi?'

'It was pleasant, my dear.' He looked up at his wife, who always greeted his arrival from the top of the stairs.

'Your face is pale.'

'I ... I had that vision again.' He started up the stairs. The chandelier above him twinkled, the polished banister gleamed. 'As I came round the corner, you know – after the row of houses down there – as I walked, just as the house appeared, it looked ruined, desolate. I kept seeing empty windows, fallen roofs, no matter how much I blinked, no matter which side of the road I walked on. All the glass panes were gone, and today, today one shutter hung loose, squeaking and slamming in the wind. One shutter – the only one left.'

'Luigi, that is horrible.'

'I keep receiving these glimpses into a future when the house will be but a skeleton of what it is today. A ruin.'

She took his arm, led him into the green drawing room, and poured him a brandy. 'It is your anxiety that does this. Don't be anxious. Prasseide and I are quite happy.'

'She has no friends, Marianna.'

'She has us. She has the maestro, who comes to teach her the harp. You should have heard her today. She played the Swiss songs, all six, and it was perfect. Even the maestro clapped.'

'Beethoven.'

'Yes.'

'Does he not flinch to see her face?'

She shook her head. 'That man is a treasure. He does not pretend not to mind ... he really does not worry about her appearance, but delights in her talent. For him, it's the music.'

'Does she ...'

His wife knew what he was going to say. 'She loves playing the harp. She is getting so very good at it. It delights her.'

He downed the last of his brandy and sat there, forlorn and numb with melancholy. 'Perhaps we should take a trip. How would you like a visit to Mondello – a week or so?'

It was at Mondello, in Sicily, that Prasseide took to wearing a veil. It was a short white veil of muslin she embroidered herself with silk dots. She attached it to her straw summer hat and gathered it artfully so it hid her face.

Neither her mother, nor the girl who travelled with them to see to their wardrobes and cases, nor her father made any comments. They tactfully refrained from even staring or nodding. It was not mentioned, and the girl made herself a number of veils, which she always wore outside or on rides in the carriage, and even now when the maestro visited, she wore a veil. She devised a little bonnet to which she would fasten a length of lace or tulle that matched her outfit, and was never again seen without it.

'I shall ask the coachman to take me down to the sea,' she would say sometimes.

On one occasion, Marianna was embroidering in the gazebo, listening to the swishing of the branches on a windy afternoon, thinking she should return to the house. At the garden door, her daughter stood, in her grey suit, with a grey hat and a black veil over her face. Marianna did not like the black veil. 'Are you taking a ride in the *karrozzin*?'

'I don't know. Sometimes I feel I get dressed for nothing.'

'Oh. Oh – shall we go together?'

'No, no – I'll get Rosa to get the coachman.'

'He's getting old and tired, Prasseide. Perhaps young Karist can take you. His son; he's very possibly old enough, and capable. I've seen him hold that whip rather proudly.'

So Karist the young son would take her on outings that gradually grew longer and more ambitious. They would break away from the Żejtun road, and even go down to the pretty bay in Birzebbuġa. But her melancholy, which started with that black veil, was never truly broken.

Marianna would find her staring at the mural on the landing.

'What is it, my darling?'

'Sometimes it's better than looking at the real scene from the side terrace. Sometimes it's better than looking through the columns of the gazebo.' In the corner of one of her eyes, a tear hung on the lopsided eyelid. Her mouth drooped, and her uneven teeth seemed even more disfigured than usual.

Her mother did not mention that the mural was the cause of all their misfortune. She tried to distract her daughter. 'Papa is taking us to Paris.'

'To Paris!'

'There are performances by Alphonse Hasselmans which he thinks you will love to attend. I think we should accept.'

'They say he plays the harp like a real angel. How would they know what a real angel sounds like? Or whether there are any angels at all?'

'You don't believe in …'

'There cannot be any heaven, Mama.'

Marianna lowered her head and turned away.

'There cannot be any God, Mama.'

'Why, you …'

'I was twelve, Mama. How would God strike down anyone with a disease like this at twelve, to be doomed forever? And children died. Papa told us. In Marsa, in Valletta, in Floriana, and even in the three cities, children died when their fathers brought home smallpox from the docks.'

'Hush, you will …'

Prasseide's eyes flashed with an anger her mother had never seen before. '… bring down a curse upon us? I am already doomed and cursed. *Seħitni xihadd.*'

Marianna's quick intake of breath was audible as they descended the main staircase. Not only did Prasseide talk of curses, but she said the words in Maltese. The language carried such power. It was the language of the land. It was hewn into the bedrock of the island.

Marianna understood enough of it to be shocked. *'You were cursed by someone?'*

Beautiful rays of sunlight entered the arched windows to the twin balconies, and the Cyclops window sent a shaft of pure gold to rest on the mural on the other side. 'My darling girl ...'

'But I shall persist. I will endure. We shall go to Paris, and when we come back, no one will move me from here.' Her eyes flashed again. 'I shall be here until that mural is no more.'

Marianna knew that Lazzaro had prepared the surface well, and that it would last forever. So she took heart that she would always enjoy her daughter's company. She would never be taken from her, in the way that other mothers saw their daughters married off to some distant husband, to be caught up in childbirth and what amounted domestic servitude. Even with a squadron of servants, women were imprisoned, for a lifetime of restrictions. Men could march off, presented with an array of choices, and women were restricted to the same fate as their mothers and grandmothers before them.

'At least you are not to be married off. On that you can rely. Papa too would like you with us. Not too many women have that choice.' The older woman paused. 'If we do make unusual choices, like the arts, or performance, we are treated in the same way as prostitutes.'

'What?' Prasseide turned from the mural, startled at her mother's choice of words.

'I'm sorry. I was thinking aloud. Life is hard, Prasseide, but I am sorry you think it is God who dooms us.'

'Of course not.' She smiled and took her mother's arm. 'There is no God.'

The patient mother raised a hand to her forehead. Scandalized, shocked, she tried to stay calm. 'Do not let your father hear you talk like that. He would call it blasphemy.'

'My father is not the one who is shocked by my opinions, Mama. It is you.'

'Oh. Prasseide.'

'We might never go to church, but I sense it in you. You do whisper a prayer every now and then.'

'You lived, my darling. You survived.'

'I have an ugly face. I have an ugly countenance. You gave me an ugly name.'

Marianna stood immobile. 'Stop. Stop, Prasseide! It is a beautiful name ... after the Greek goddess Praxedes, who was a benefactor of the poor and the unfortunate. It means *with good intent*.'

There was a momentary silence in which they looked at each other.

'Well then – you must heed my opinions, because you are convinced of my good *intent*.' Prasseide let go her mother's arm and turned, skirts swishing. For an instant, the veil clung to her face, and she resembled, to her mother's mind, a Greek statue she had seen somewhere. *Oh, that face.*

The younger woman was already halfway down the stairs. She would run out to the gazebo and watch for owls. In her mind, she was steadfast in her opinion. She was cursed, someone had cursed her and her form, her face and her figure, and she would forever walk the staircase she had just descended so rapidly, and grieve for beauty in the rooms beyond her father's complicated stair locks, seeking in vain a destiny she could never have.

*

Eleven

Flagstones

The old professor was tired. He still travelled to Valletta regularly by *karrozzin*, these days with young Karist coaxing the horse onward with the clicking sound he made in the side of his mouth. They had recently refurbished the tack, which meant all the new leatherwork on horse and rig now gleamed with a new glint in the sun on their way out in the early morning; and in the lamplight on their return very late at night.

They would interrupt the journey in Tarxien, where the doctor would alight at a small coffee shop and partake of a peasant's beaker of red wine or two. He sent one out to Karist, who waited patiently at his post.

Tarxien was quiet at night. The doctor knew that the resident doctor, who was a student at the university at the same time as him, and whose patronage by patients far and wide was something legendary, lived in a large house whose woodwork and balcony were painted dark blue, behind the massive church. The two physicians had lost touch when Luigi went to study in Scotland, but they still exchanged salutations and pleasantries when they met in Valletta, from time to time. Nevertheless, he would not break his journey with a visit, even when invited. A note arrived one winter, and read tersely:

> *Dear Luigi*
> *Your coachman takes you regularly past my house. You will do me an honour to break your journey on any evening of your choice, for refreshment and a rest.*
> *Salvatore Buhagiar*

They went past his house many an evening, when they sought refreshment at that tiny coffee shop, where light spilled onto the road, and tradesmen and peasants gathered, before darkness drove them home to their wives. Luigi was reluctant to start an intimate friendship with someone who would expect their families to be included in a round of visits, especially when their parish *festa* was on. Marianna and Prasseide would not delight in invitations of that kind, and refusal would cause the kind of social brushoff that was intolerable to the doctor's mind. So the response, equally terse, was worded with some difficulty, to suggest polite indefinite postponement of the 'honour'. Another invitation was never received.

It was even more awkward when they heard Doctor Buhagiar and his family were moving to Żejtun. The men remained cordial, but a friendship never developed.

They clip-clopped, tonight like every other, onward on the Żejtun road, reaching the bend where the doctor averted his eyes and stayed snug behind the leather curtain, lest he see once more the devastation and wreckage in a vision he wanted never to experience again.

'*Ara x'kokka dik!*' An involuntary exclamation from the young coachman made the doctor lean out to address him.

He was just in time to see an enormous owl fly across their path. Perfectly visible in some ghostly light, it was speckled, with a huge wingspan. It turned its head to gaze with yellow eyes in Luigi's direction, and he shivered. 'An owl, Karist. That's all it is. An owl.'

'It came from the *girna* at Villa Marnisi.' His arm, which shook a bit, pointed out across the fields to their right.

'A fortunate owl. One the hunters missed in their eagerness to shoot anything and everything that flies.'

The young coachman shook his head. 'Not fortunate for us at all. At all. It's a bad omen, for such a big bird to cross your path after the moon is up. It flew across the face of the moon.'

'Come on, Karist. Get us home.'

Discussed briefly at the dinner table that night, the owl was not suggested by the doctor to be an omen of any kind.

'There is a wonderful book on the birds of our islands in the downstairs bookcase, in my study. I looked up Maltese owls and found the huge bird was a *Kokka tax-Xagħri*.'

'I love owls.' Prasseide put down her dessert spoon and looked up. 'But they are not frequent visitors. I have seen a large one twice – probably the same one, Papa.'

'When was that, my dear girl?'

'The last time was a fortnight ago. I stood on the balcony of the drawing room.'

'Out there, at night?'

She laughed. 'Just after dark, to see the great moon.'

'Ah yes – I remember. The enormous red moon over the fields. It casts a powerful light.'

His daughter nodded, dabbed a napkin to her lips, and restored her veil over her face. 'And the owl flew across, from the Marnisi fields to our gazebo. It felt like a sign.'

'An omen?' Marianna's frown spelled fear.

'We do not speak of omens or premonitions.' The doctor was quick in an attempt to halt the conversation.

'Like we do not speak of God.' Prasseide's voice was slightly hoarse.

He was glad he could not see his daughter's eyes under the veil, because he knew they would be full of a new kind of bitterness.

The owl was well forgotten a month later, when Luigi returned home from a hard day at the Valletta clinic to hear arguing voices from the house. It had never happened before. He usually came home to Marianna standing at the top of the stairs, welcoming him. She took pains to have all the lamps lit, and the house quiet and serene.

Tonight, his daughter's raised voice rang out, upset at something her mother seemed unable to put right. 'Why? Why can't I go through the gates? Where are the keys? Are you keeping them from me?'

The doctor looked up from the hallway. 'Good evening, my dears. Something seems to be wrong. I could hear your voice from behind the leather curtain of the *karrozzin*, Prasseide.' It was a soft rebuke, but a rebuke nevertheless.

'I am so glad you are home, Luigi.' Marianna's eyes sent him a tacit message of sadness, a flash of wordless warning of their daughter's mood. 'Prasseide would like to sit in the small room at the back. And we cannot open the gates on the stairs.'

He ascended quickly, patting his pocket for the keys. 'Why the back room, my dear? Why tonight?'

'Do I have to detail my wishes and movements to the entire household? I am of age. I have reached my majority. I am ... I have ... oh!' She made an angry sound of frustration, stamped a foot, and turned away from her father, who hurried up another flight, still patting his pocket. He stopped at the gate. 'The keys! I thought they were on me.'

Marianna raised a hand to her mouth. 'Oh, so did we. And Prasseide thought I was forbidding her access.'

The sad look in Marianna's eyes raised the doctor's ire. 'Do not upset your mother like this, Prasseide. You are becoming impatient and abrupt. Your abrasive behaviour and words upset your mother. I will not have it.' He felt all the pockets in his suit. 'And the keys are missing. This is even more upsetting.'

The keys to the gates were nearly always on his person. What had happened to them? Those gates were necessary, because his impressive ivory collection was in a special room upstairs; a room replete with glass cases of every description, which held a wealth of pieces from all over the world. Some were as old as civilization itself. Others as new and inventive as artists had become in recent years. 'I hope no one has been at my collection.'

'All we need to do is find the keys.'

'Summon Karist. Tell him to bring his brothers.'

'Shall we not wait for the light of day? Tomorrow ...'

The doctor took a deep breath. 'Tomorrow will be too late. Now. Right now. Call Karist.'

So the servants' rest was interrupted, and a great search took place all over house and grounds. Searching in the dark was not an undertaking the superstitious folk liked. They crossed themselves many times, and held their fists clenched with index and little fingers extended. *'Agħmel qrun, Karist!'*

The man was bade to form a horned fist, and he looked inside the *girna* in the field, with the scent of sandalwood from the house giving way to jasmine of the garden in his nostrils. Reluctantly, he ascended the five steps of the gazebo, where it was even darker than on the path. He frightened a dove which fluttered past him. 'Oh!'

Getting on his knees, he felt the entire floor inch by inch, and his hand finally struck something that jangled in the quiet of the night.

'I found them! The keys are found!' He ran to the house, where he was rewarded with a florin by the doctor.

'They must have fallen out of my pocket on Sunday.'

'Yes, Doctor.'

'Thank you, Karist. Thank your brothers.'

The gates on the stairs were opened, and the doctor hurried to check his collection room. His gasp of dismay could be heard halfway down the stairs. 'Oh no! Oh no!'

Marianna joined him, out of breath. She saw that one glass case was smashed, and that something was taken from it, because it was half empty. 'Oh no, Luigi. What is missing?'

'The Chinese carvings. Three of them. The Sleeping Buddha, the large hollow tusk, and the beautiful bridge – even their wooden plinths are gone.' He turned, his shoulders bent and his face ashen. 'They are priceless. Irreplaceable. But they are also unique, so they cannot be sold, if I hurry and make the theft known.'

He strode past her and ran down two flights of stairs, and soon, the clanging of the bell on the roof could be heard. It rang out into the night, over the fields, through the windows of the district. It rang a melancholic peal of urgency; a frenzied tolling that woke up anyone in the vicinity of the Żejtun road.

Prasseide stood on the stairs, helpless, immobile, as her father flew about, ordering servants to do this and that, making sure that someone kept pulling the taut wire that ran through the wall up to the bell on the roof. One of the servants was stationed at the bell pull.

'Keep it ringing!'

There were shouts outside.

'Who is that?'

Someone called up from the hallway below.

'What is it? Who is it?'

'The gardener from the Villa Marnisi is here, Doctor. He wants to know if everyone is safe.'

'Everyone is safe. Bid him to tell the baron we are all safe, but three of my carvings are gone.'

Karist would have to drive the *karrozzin* out at first light, to summon someone from the police station in Żejtun.

'We are so far from everyone, from everything.' It was the first time anyone heard Marianna rue their isolation.

It took a char-a-banc, full of constables from Floriana, to eventually find a solution to the mysterious theft from behind locked gates. The police commissioner sent as many men as he could spare, after about thirty hours, and in the broad light of day, with constables walking through the district questioning everyone they met, a culprit was finally found.

People said the barefooted boy hung his head at the police station in Żejtun, and admitted he was very stupid to return the keys to where he had found them on the flagstones in the gazebo.

'And just as stupid to push the valuable carvings underneath your bed.' The irate commissioner now saw his task was reduced to the ridiculous.

'What?'

'What were you doing trespassing in the garden of the Villa Sans Souci, young fellow?'

'Where?'

'The house from where you stole these three carvings. What were you doing there?'

'Looking for cigar stubs, of course.' Was it not obvious? He shrugged, and looked with wide dim eyes into those of the policeman. 'Gentlemen throw away their cigars with a good few puffs left in them. That little garden house often has two or three lying about.'

'And the rest ... just opportunism? Eh? Tell me!'

'What?'

'Never mind.'

*

Twelve

Limestone building

Talking to Meg on the phone seemed to improve things. Philip placed his mobile on the arm of the sofa after ending the call, feeling pleased with the conversation. For the first time in months, they had had a nice lively chat. Perhaps taking a break made him feel less uptight.

Perhaps absence did make the heart grow fonder. He looked at his empty beer glass and shook his head at the cliché. Perhaps having a beer or two before and during the calls to his wife made it all better. He could not tell. The time on the front of the tiny phone told him it was too late now to attempt another visit to Villa Sans Souci, even though it was what he wanted to do most.

But it might not be too late to try for a fresh tuna and caper pizza in Birzebbuġa. Thinking of the huge pizza on its round plate made him hungry. He had eaten one before, after seeing it on a neighbouring table, and saying to the waiter, 'I'll have one of those, please.' It felt like a year ago, but could only have been a few days.

He was cutting into the delicious crust inside of thirty minutes from ending his call to Meg, and was still cheerful about her mood. 'I might very well come out to you for a visit – is there room for me at your flat?'

'Plenty of room!' He had exclaimed, surprised at himself. Now that was a turnaround he had not expected. He had come out all on his own to get a much needed break from *everything*. But it might be nice to show her around, and rekindle something from all those years ago, when they had spent their honeymoon discovering the islands. No doubt the kids would look after themselves while she was gone.

Neither of them was a child any more. Where had the time gone?

'Are you still interested in that house?' It was a gruffer voice than Meg's, and not distant and tinny like hers had sounded on the phone, but right at his shoulder, from someone just out of sight. But Philip knew who it was.

'It's Charl Emmaus, Philip.'

'Yes, I remember you.'

'This time you got to a table first.'

There was little Philip could do without being rude but invite her to take the other chair. Luckily, he had enjoyed most of the pizza in peace.

'I have good news. Since you are so interested, and so aware of the condition of the ...'

'Are you talking about Villa Sans Souci? The place is a dump. Anyone who buys that place would have to spend a fortune making it habitable. I'm not interested in it. Not in the way you might think, anyway.'

She patted her hair in a needless gesture, and dabbed at the side of her mouth. 'Wait until I tell you the kind of money they're asking.'

'Not interested, Charl.'

'You'll be pleasantly surprised.'

'Not interested, Charl.'

'Look – I'll state the price, leave my card on your table, and you can either get in touch or not. How does that sound to you?'

'And I thought you were trying to flog me a cruise, Charlotte.' Philip laughed.

The woman's face stayed serious. 'Charl. Call me Charl. A cruise? A *cruise*?' She looked to the left and right, and then leaned to see if someone might be listening behind her. It was a parody meant to imply secrecy. 'Now that you mention it, I can get you a really good price ... exceptional, on the Magenta Line. On the *Nettuno*. Are you all alone? Yes – single cabin, or shared. It leaves on Tuesday for Piraeus and Corfu and ...'

Philip shook his head and took up his wine glass. 'Ha ha. I can't believe this. Well, I do believe it.'

'No cruise?'

He shook his head.

Charl Emmaus stood, pointed at her business card on the table, raised one eyebrow on that prominent forehead in a dramatic way, and minced out of the restaurant. At the door, she twirled round and made her way back.

Philip watched her return with annoyance in his head, which throbbed with something like a tension headache. What could she want now?

'Two hundred thousand.' She turned and left before he could say another word.

The figure stayed in the doctor's mind all night. Two hundred thousand. It was nothing. It was as cheap as a property could get anywhere on the island, and he wondered whether or not Charl Emmaus was trying to tempt him with some foolish sum, a mere temptation before additions and increments where made for this and that.

In the morning, he was convinced the number was made up just to keep him interested. Driving to the house was second nature; the car knew the way. The road from Żejtun was much less busy than the one between Xgħajra and Żejtun, giving him the opportunity to tune out and think about money again.

Meg would think he was crazy. Meg would start talking about divorce. It was stupid to even consider buying Villa Sans Souci. It was a property with marked problems. And being haunted was the least of the problems he could see. Replacing roofs and ceilings was not cheap.

Pulling up at the house, parking in the narrow gravel strip outside, however, almost changed his mind. In bright sunlight, he could see so much potential in that limestone building. A sign, swinging in the sea breeze, reading *Philip and Meg's – The Place to Stay* in green and gold, might bring in holidaymakers by the dozen.

What was he thinking? Meg would hate the whole idea. Still, it was not too far-fetched to imagine her filling the hostess role and preparing lovely breakfasts, while he looked after the rest. It would be such a change from the medical practice. If only.

What he should do was take a walk down to Marsaxlokk and have a good look at the bay, and tentatively entice Meg for a break with him, and they could decide on this life-changing move together.

Really? A life-changing move. He shook his head, impatient and bemused by his own daydreams.

'Look – stranger things have happened.' Talking to himself was not that strange, not in Marsaxlokk.

It was an easy walk down Żejtun Road, and soon Philip found himself in a bustling seaside town. Colourful and full of tourists, it was sun-drenched and smelled of the sea and fish. Delightful, just the right distance from the house. In easy reach of all this, it stood, and yet peaceful. He bought an enormous ice-cream cone and paced about, promising himself he would take some photos and send them to Meg.

The church stood on top of a semi-circular flight of shallow steps, bounded by a balustrade to form a forecourt. He gazed upward and thought it must be an unchanged scene, one the original occupants of his villa might have looked upon.

'How old is this church?' He addressed a man in a cloth cap who sat outside a small café.

'Very old.'

Philip grinned. How could he get him to say more?

'It's not as old as some others.' The words came from another man, who promptly sat on the bench in the sun too. 'And it's been restored. The belfries are not the original ones. And the façade is hardly a hundred years old.'

'And the priests are old, too.' The older man would not be outdone.

'About as old as Villa Sans Souci?'

Both men fell silent.

'Is it? Are they about the same age?'

'We cannot mention them in the same breath, can we sir? A house like that and a church.' He crossed himself.

'It was a *burdell*.' The older one leaned forward, displaying a brilliant denture. He smiled widely. 'A house of ill-repute! Now it's a ruin. Serve them right, I say.'

'Do you remember the brothel?'

'We know nothing,' the younger man said quickly.

Philip rose and plunged a hand into his jeans pocket. 'You might remember if I buy you a beer. Hopleaf?'

The men looked at each other with inexpressive faces. They turned and nodded at the doctor in exactly the same way.

The cheap but excellent beer made them both loquacious. They burst with information that complemented and contradicted each other.

'No – she was not French ... she was a Sicilian actress.'

'Not Sicilian. Someone said she was from some volcanic island.'

'There's a huge volcano in Sicily, remember?'

'No ... no. Ah! Stromboli ... that's where. Stromboli.'

They both rocked with laughter.

'Who? What? What's so funny?'

'The wife of the man who had the house built. She was from Stromboli. Perhaps that's why she was a bit *strumblata*!'

Mirth ceased their faces and made them nod and rock again.

'What? What does that mean?'

'Crazy. A bit unhinged.' The younger man slapped the table top. 'She wasn't his wife, either. My aunt says they were not married in a church ... you know, like foreigners do.'

'So they could not be in heaven now, sir, hee hee hee.'

'And they say there was a daughter who was funny in the head. It wasn't the wife. That's what I remember.'

'We know for sure one of them is nowhere near heaven. She's right here.'

Philip sat forward, with an elbow on each knee. 'In Marsaxlokk?'

The men laughed. 'Not down here by the sea, no. Up at the house. People say one of the um ... *girls* at the house threw herself off the terrace and died on the flagstones in the garden.'

The older man grunted. 'Don't invent things. Listen, sir – it was like this. One of the prostitutes was murdered. Someone took her head right off her neck and ...'

'... and she now walks on the terrace under the moon.'

'Really?' Philip wanted to keep them talking.

'All that is gossip and rubbish.'

'It's the honest truth. People have seen her, in white, walking up and down behind the columns – stone columns, that are still standing. You can see them from the road.'

'It's local folklore.' The doctor suggested something likely. It would bring forth more tattle.

'It's dreamed up by the locals for tourists, see?'

'But some of it is true!'

'No, it isn't, you old fool.'

'Yes it is. Why is the house still vacant after all these years? Why is it a ruin? Every time someone makes repairs it returns to its old state overnight.' He snapped old fingers. 'Just like that. The window glass all exploded in one day. They fixed one section of roof, and it came down the next day. The stairs ... same thing. The only thing left, which gives an idea of how grand it was, is the *gaziba*.'

'Good for picnics, eh?'

The old man looked at Philip with watery eyes. 'Are you joking? A nice picnic is the last thing you can have in that condemned place. Bats will come out at you. You will see ghosts. Try it!'

'What – in the middle of the day?'

'Some people say it's always night in that garden. Few are brave enough to find out if it's true or not. There was elegance and glory there once – now they cannot even find the back staircase. Or the secret room with the treasure.'

'Treasure?'

'Coins. Coins and banknotes, some say. A roomful.'

The old man nodded. 'Some say sculptures. Beautiful naked women ... statues. Like in Greece. Do you know who will tell you about this? Jessie. Jessie *tal-midħna*.'

The young man explained. '*Tal-midħna* is their family nickname. It means mill people. Their ancestors had a flourmill up the road, years ago. Now they run a haberdashery. Jessie is the great granddaughter of the dressmaker who used to go to the house, in the old days. Before the war, eh? Oh yes, well before the Great War, even. No one really remembers anything, sir.'

'Where does she ... where can I find her – this sounds promising.'

The younger man squinted against the sun, looking into Philip's face as he rose. 'Don't promise yourself anything. Thank you for the beer. Look – you don't have to go far to find Jessie. She's behind the counter of her shop ...' he consulted his wristwatch, and craned his neck to check it with the church clock across the way. '... until about one. If you hurry you'll

The White Lady of Marsaxlokk

catch her. It's on St Catherine Street, behind the church. Go – hurry!'

It was dark inside the shop. Philip waited for his eyes to adjust to the gloomy interior. 'Jessie?'

'Who wants her?'

Before he had time to answer, a young boy at the counter shouted through a backdoor, and a woman came out, wiping her hands on a brilliant white apron. 'You're the one asking about the house?'

The doctor was struck speechless. How could word travel that fast? He knew villages had some sort of lightning telegraph that travelled faster than one could walk, but this was quite remarkable. Someone must have texted her a quick message. 'How could you possibly know?'

'This is Marsaxlokk, sir – no secrets. Except the recipe of Pawlu's peas and anchovy filling, for *pastizzi*. He bakes so well people come from Żejtun to buy them.'

'And from Għaxaq.' The boy was still in the doorway.

'Go and have your lunch! What are you still doing here?' She turned to Philip. 'My great grandmother, and my grandmother, died when I was little, sir. I don't know much.'

'Have you ever been in the house? When it was …?'

'Are you joking? No way. Besides, at one point it was occupied. You don't just walk in, do you? There was a couple … I think the wife was English. They had a little what-you-call-it, like a hotel, and that was when I was little. And even then they said their guests used to see some *ħares* or other. Let me tell you what …'

'I know what it means.'

'Oh – so you have been speaking to many people. Perhaps you want to buy the land? They want so much money for it … because it comes with extras!' She laughed hard and held on to the counter. Just as full of mirth as the men in the square. 'Ah, I shouldn't laugh.' Her peals of laughter rang in the dark shop. '*Ajma* – I shouldn't laugh. It comes with a ghost, see?'

'Something money can't buy.'

'Oh, no – on the contrary ...' she giggled and wiped her hands needlessly on the white apron. 'Something money can't get rid of! Ha ha. If it could, that house would be done up and worth at least a million, like the Marnisi one. Have you been to see it? It's quite amazing. No *fatati* there.' She described the other villa, which was set back from the Żejtun road. 'Blue shutters, large stone urns full of geraniums, restored paving stones, and oiled wooden beams inside. Oiled – do you know the cost of restoring and oiling beams? Someone said they have Persian rugs and a beautiful wall clock. *Tal-Lira*.'

'That sounds interesting.'

'Those clocks, sir, are interesting. They are real antiques now – they were called Pound Clocks, and do you know why?'

The doctor shook his head. But the boy, who was still hanging around the doorway, interrupted the conversation. 'They were not always called Pound Clocks at all. Lira does mean pound, as in the old money. But Lira also means lyre.'

'The instrument?'

His mother frowned at him. 'Tell this man your story, then *go and eat your lunch*!'

Smiling, the boy leapt up and sat on the counter, swinging his legs. He could not have been older than eleven or twelve. 'Yes. Some called them Lyre Clocks, because the bottom decoration of the case was shaped like a lyre – you see, they were wall clocks – they didn't stand on a table or anything. And some called them Pound Clocks, either because they didn't know the real name, or because they thought that the ... what's that thing that goes tick-tock, from side to side, like this?' He swung an arm.

'The pendulum.'

'That's right, *pendlu* – it was gilded, and round,

like a gold coin, a *Lira*. What's the word ... sovereign! Sometimes with the King's head on it, going tick-tock, tick-tock, back and forth, behind the glass, behind a special glazed and gilded door.'

'And they're expensive?'

Jessie raised her chin at the boy and he hopped off the counter and out the doorway.

She continued in her son's place. 'The reproductions are expensive enough – all that gold leaf, all that work. It's real artisan's work. But the original antiques? First of all they are impossible to find, and then, they are now worth literally many thousands.'

'Do you know if there was one at the house?'

'What – the villa? There was no such thing as a grand house without one, in those days. But let me tell you,' she started to giggle again. 'An antique Pound Clock would be worth much more than the house is, today. Ha ha! The owners would happily swap you their house and land for a real *Arloġġ tal-Lira*!'

Philip saw that the locals thought the place might be worthless. 'What would someone foreign, say, someone who did not believe in ghosts, have to pay for it then?'

'Someone crazy? Someone like you, sir?'

'Someone insane like me, yes.' It was his turn to laugh.

'Don't even think of paying a cent more than four hundred thousand.'

So it did have a market value, after all.

She dropped her voice to a whisper and told him the story of a disfigured girl, kept inside by her parents, never meeting a soul. 'My great grandmother would tell my father, as a young boy, how ugly she was. How her skin was wrinkled and uneven. How she had craters as large as coins in her forehead, cheeks, neck, and arms, and how she could not shut one of her eyes. Ever.' She nodded sadly. 'So she had to sleep in complete darkness. And ...' she lowered her voice to a lower whisper. '... she had a fondness for owls and bats.'

'Really?'

'That's why people around here started calling them *Tal-pipistrell*. Pipistrell means bat.'

'Does everyone have a nickname?'

'Almost. With so many people who have the same surname ... in my father's day people had families of twelve and fourteen children sometimes. All Borg, or Falzon, or Sammut, or Meilaq. A village would be full of them.'

'My name is Falzon.'

'Ha ha ha! See? See?' She raised a corner of the apron to the corner of her eye. 'You have a sense of humour – perhaps you should buy that house. But let me go on ... they eventually found her a husband. From very far away. He could not have been aware of how she looked.'

'Goodness. How did that end?'

'Well ... it ended with her death, of course. But she found no rest, sir.' Jessie crossed herself. 'And don't try to prove me wrong by spending the night there. You'll be terrified out of your wits.'

*

Thirteen

Lodgings in Valletta

'The king is coming to Malta. We should spend a few days in Valletta.'

'Not with your cousins? Prasseide will never go with us. She will never accept. She will demand to be left behind.' Marianna pulled her mouth into a disappointed line. 'And I do so want to catch a glimpse of the king. Oh – if only. How exciting it would be, Luigi.'

'He is coming on his yacht, the *Victoria and Albert*. It has steam engines – and someone said as many as three hundred sailors on board!'

Marianna placed a pensive hand under her chin. 'Oh – it would be so lovely.'

'You're right. Our daughter would not like the ... lack of privacy at my cousin's home. What if I took lodgings? For a week?'

'In Valletta – with a royal visit imminent? Impossible! Every available room will be taken.'

But Luigi achieved the impossible. He got one of the valets from the Casino Maltese, an exclusive men's club, to bring him information about suitable lodgings, and was rewarded – for the exorbitant cost of three florins to grease the man's palm – with the possibility of a week's lodging on one floor of a beautiful house at Santa Barbara Bastion.

'That's not all,' he announced to his wife and daughter at dinner that day. 'I have also secured tickets for a performance of *La Forza del Destino* at the opera house. With the king in attendance!'

'Oh! King Edward and the opera, and *Verdi*, all in one night. But I thought the place was destroyed by fire.'

The doctor nodded. 'It's has been rebuilt – restored to its original glory. I have walked past it myself. The scaffolding is down. It is ready to receive patrons, including royalty.'

'And us.' Marianna was excited.

'I will not reside with the Valletta cousins.' The girl straightened her back and took on a stubborn stance.

'No – no need to, Prasseide. I have just told you, I secured the whole floor of a large house – just for us. Karist can lodge with the servants. It's all arranged.'

'Is this all not costing a fortune, just because ...?'

'Oh bah!' The doctor waved a hand, as if chasing away some insect. 'Bah, and bah again. It will be such a diversion. Such an entertainment. We will all remember it for a long time.'

'And we can have opera dresses made? Is there time?'

'There is time.' He sat back with a magnanimous expression making his face glow. This might be a sign of things taking a turn for the better. Prasseide looked almost happy. Very nearly content. She had something to which she could look forward.

Marianna looked at her daughter, and saw she responded to generosity. She thrived when kindness was dealt her way.

Her eyes shone. 'When?'

'In April. In early April. The king will arrive in Valletta, he will sail into Grand Harbour, all the way from Portsmouth, via Lisbon and Gibraltar.'

'Oh! How exciting. And will Queen Alexandra also come?'

'I think so.'

Their excitement grew from that point.

It was a marvellous week, spent in a flurry of anticipating where the royal couple might appear, and getting there by *karrozzin*. The narrow Valletta streets were crowded with people, some who travelled for days from distant towns and villages, on carts, drays, carriages and char-a-bancs. There were also numerous sailors in white, with jaunty caps at an angle. The main thoroughfare, Kingsway, was decorated for the occasion, and even a glimpse of the royal carriage and entourage was cause for cries of joy and applause.

Prasseide wore her veil everywhere, and it was gratifying to see she enjoyed the whole event. Allowing a lighter shade of purple for her opera outfit, she had to admit, standing in front of a cheval mirror with her mother at the door, that lilac was not a bad choice.

'The queen is setting the fashion wherever she goes. That stylish hair – it must take hours every morning.'

Hr mother smiled. 'How would you like...?'

'A waste of time, it would be, for me and my hair, behind my veils.' She adjusted her mauve hat and delicately tinted lilac veil.

There was no more to be said on the subject of hairstyles, Marianna saw that plainly. 'You are enjoying this, Prasseide.'

She stamped her foot and growled. 'Oh, how I wish I was called Jane or Susan or Penelope.'

'What! They are such ...'

'Such *English* names! People are giving their children English names. And not family names, like the coachman's family. His son is *also* called Karist.'

'It means Eucharist.'

'Bah! Everyone in Sliema is calling their children names with no meaning.'

'How do you know? And ... but ... they are not Christian names. Prasseide ... your father and I chose so carefully.'

She turned from the mirror. 'Mine is not a Christian name either! It had to be preceded by Maria at my baptism, or the priest would never have ... if I cannot be Clare or Ruby, can I not be called Mary, then?'

'*Mary*?'

She strode to the table and rustled the

newspaper. 'Look – look! People in Sliema do everything in English. Their birth announcements in the *Chronicle* show their babies are being named Arthur and Laurence and Margaret and Helen.'

Marianna smiled. 'Well, *Mary* – the carriage is waiting. Papa is taking us on a little tour around the port and Floriana.'

If there had been no veil in the way, Marianna would have glimpsed her daughter's tentative, lopsided smile.

*

Fourteen

Green drawing room

The professor's grief was immense. He stood at the top of the stairs. Walked down slowly, and turned in the hallway to look upward. He would never see her stand there again, all in yellow. Or in green, or deep blue, or pink.

Marianna suffered a massive stroke on their return from Valletta, early in the morning on the Sunday following the King's visit, and died in his arms. Before he could summon Karist, before he could shout for Prasseide. It took a minute. A minute or two, and she was gone. One instant asleep next to him, the next babbling something incoherent, and falling unconscious in the next, her limbs twisted in the characteristic abnormal posture, impossible to revive.

'Me, a doctor, unable to revive my beloved,' he said later to the baron from the Villa Marnisi. 'Unable to do anything. Helpless. I could not help her, I couldn't.'

'Luigi, do not blame yourself.'

'There was not even time to summon Doctor Buhagiar from Żejtun.'

Prasseide was disconsolate. Nothing could help her either. She paced her rooms. She paced her mother's sitting room, in tears for days. An aunt came from Valletta; her father's cousin, filled with concern but visibly discomforted by the girl's disfigurement. She could not bring herself to look into her niece's face.

There was a month of confusion, heartache, and miserable despondency.

'Mama!' She cried into a mass of pillows on a bed of tangled stained sheets. 'Mama – I can call all I want. You will never answer again.' Her wailing brought Rosa, the maid, to her side, but nothing could console her.

'The only one who called me Mary.' She was reduced to mumbling incoherencies and maddened phrases, over and over, through the day and night. She exhausted herself.

'You will make yourself sick, Prasseide.'

'I am sick. I have been ill for many years. Sick inside. Half-dead. My only companion is gone ... and she was always worried about what would become of me. She worries no longer. *Mama!*'

'Prasseide!'

'There is no one left.'

'Not even I, my dear?'

She rose and gave him her back. 'You'll see. I'll see – you will abandon me yet.'

If her father could see her eyes behind that delicately embroidered veil, he would have seen her gaze venomously at his face. He did not think of countering her resentment, her unhappy wrath, with generosity of spirit.

There was a man in the upstairs drawing room when Prasseide was summoned by a maid to see her father on the feast day of Our Lady of Pompeii.

The servants were all given the day off. Only old Rosa stayed at home. The sounds of revelry, fireworks, marching bands and cheering could be heard from the garden. She had not heard anyone arrive.

A man in grey. A man in grey in the green drawing room. She saw his form in one of the mirrors between the windows before she entered.

The girl took a quick step backward. 'Get my bonnet, Rosa. Why did you not say Papa had company? Fetch my bonnet and veil. Quick!'

'I thought you heard his carriage, *sinjura*.'

'Do not think. Thinking does nothing. My bonnet!'

In three minutes, she entered, graceful, in a

gliding movement of which her mother would have been proud.

'Prasseide, this is Mister Peter Ellul.'

She did not move forward to take the man's held out hand. 'You must be from Sliema, with a name like Peter.'

'Birkirkara.'

'Mister Ellul is here with excellent news. He bears brilliant tidings from Senglea. Greetings from the Little Palace.' Her father seemed nervous.

Prasseide stayed at the drawing room door. 'The Little Palace?'

'Palazzo Imbroll.'

'Greetings? Tidings? Could you mean condolences, so soon after my mother's death? Why greetings to me?' Questions tumbled from between the girl's uneven teeth, causing her to lisp with discomfort and foreboding. She had an idea what this might be about.

'My dear girl – it has been almost a year since Mama ...'

'I shall never recover. Do you understand? It could take a hundred years or longer. I shall never rise from this grief.' She looked at the newcomer's embarrassment, and repeated once more. 'Never.' She raised her chin an inch. 'So? Do you bear a message of sympathy from the Little Palace? Or is it only insults you convey?'

'I ... um ...' The man looked at the doctor, made a small helpless gesture with one hand, and quickly pushed it into a jacket pocket, only to remember his manners and pull it out again, shaking. 'Yes. The baronet Imbroll sends his deepest condolences.'

'Ah – he took his time.'

'Prasseide.' Her father too seemed helpless, unable to find words. 'There is more.'

'The baronet wishes to call on you, Miss Prasseide.'

'Miss? *Miss?* Please inform the baronet I do not

receive visitors. My mother is dead. I have assumed her place. I am to be addressed as Signora, *Sinjura*, Madame ...'

'Prasseide! The baronet has sent you a gift.'

She shivered. 'Does he really think that I lack anything? I have everything I need.'

Her father moved to a wooden crate, which stood to one side of the sofa. He folded back several sheets of paper to reveal a beautifully-executed wall clock.

'A lyre-clock! *Arloġġ tal-lira!* Why do you insult me with a gift appropriate for a bride? I do not intend to move to a new house. That is a gift for someone setting up a new home!'

She gave her father an icy look, which he would have deciphered; even through more layers of muslin than those that veiled her face that afternoon. 'I am afraid this messenger will have to return to Senglea to disappoint the baronet, who has scant knowledge of who I might be. Convey my displeasure to this nobleman, who wishes *to call on me!*'

The doctor turned to Peter Ellul, who stood there like one struck dumb. 'I am afraid, Mr Ellul, that you have come this great distance ...'

'It is fine. It's perfectly fine.' He looked at his abandoned half glass of sherry on the table near the chair from which he had risen when Prasseide entered the room. 'I shall ...' It was plain he did not know what to do about the clock.

'Goodbye, then.' Prasseide, the new mistress of Villa Sans Souci, turned and left.

She entered once more when her father was alone, thirty minutes later, all in a flurry, skirts rustling, even though they were shorter, narrower, more modern skirts, a fashion of the Edwardian era she had adapted.

'I find it hard to accept. I find it hard to comprehend. I find it impossibly hard to take in ... you are attempting to marry me off, despite all the words we both remember, that came from my mother's own lips! *Arloġġ tal-lira!*'

'There is no harm in ...'

'In trying? In trying?' There was a break in her voice; a break of despair, of extreme desolation. 'You spoke to a matchmaker! A *ħuttab!*' She uttered the Maltese word with all the loathing she could summon.

If the doctor could see her face, he would see tears running into the hollows and scars on her cheeks. She made sobbing sounds that filled the room.

The doctor could hardly speak, but he did. 'My darling daughter – I do not consider it marrying you off. Not *off* ... you ... I ... Let me tell you about the baronet.'

'There is nothing you can say about any man, any prospective match, any prospective husband, anything any matchmaker like Mr Ellul can tell us about *anyone in the Mediterranean*, let alone Malta, that would be the least bit interesting or relevant.'

'You don't understand.'

She laughed. It was a dreadful laugh, which rang and rattled on the gas chandeliers above her head, on each window pane on those glorious windows, on the glass pendants of a tall table lamp, which should have been lit a quarter of an hour ago. 'But I do understand. I understand everything. It is crystal clear.'

'Prasseide. The baronet has an affliction. He ...' How could he put it delicately? There was no other way but to state it clearly and truthfully. 'He is blind.'

Her swift intake of breath, her inhalation of shock, of humiliation, would forever live in her father's ears. Prasseide opened her mouth wide behind that pretty veil and screamed.

It was a shriek of misery, of bewilderment, and of profound and incurable rage, which went on, gaining volume, for a full minute. It was a cry that could hardly be called human.

Her father stood immobile, horrified. Tears

filled his eyes, and he never more than during that horrible minute wished for the presence of Marianna. How would he live through this? What had he done? His fingernails dug into the palms of his hands. It was awful, horrific.

Her scream died down. There was a profound silence, in which Prasseide's breathing was finally heard. She reached up and removed bonnet and veil. Her tortured face, the ugly skin, full of scars and pustule craters, her uneven mouth, revealed to the doctor one truth, which his daughter voiced.

'The blackest night, the blankest eyes, the deepest sightlessness, the most sombre darkness cannot hide this. It is who I am.'

The doctor took to heart the implacable insult he had dealt his daughter. His intention might have been kindly meant, but its real outcome was dreadful. He would never play this down; he could not pay her just reparation. It was impossible. 'I have hurt you.'

'You have more than hurt me. You have insulted me.'

'Stop. Stop! There is more to a person than how they look. Why do you think Lazzaro stayed a full three weeks longer, after the mural was finished, eh? Why do you think?'

'It would certainly not be because he enjoyed my company. It's ages ago. What could you possibly mean?'

He saw she had no notion why the artist had lingered, even though she must remember how he had followed her and Marianna around the grounds, engaging them in light conversation. She was little more than a child then.

'You seem to harbour ...'

She started from the room, and turned at the door. 'My pain is profound. My anger will never be quelled. My vengeance will descend on this house. We shall never forget this. It will haunt you unto death.' Her soft voice made it sound more appalling. 'Unto death. I shall not rest. I shall never rest.'

He heard her summon Karist and the *karrozzin*. With his hand on the shutter handle, with the window ajar against the darkness of the night, the sharp breeze from Marsaxlokk bay, and the slanting shafts of moonlight punctuated by scudding clouds, the doctor watched her being driven off at speed down the Żejtun road.

Where was she bound? Perhaps she wanted to calm herself by gazing out at the sea. Her dismay and disappointment were sharp in his heart and mind. The pain of having hurt her, even though all he wanted was for her to always be as comfortable and cared for as possible, thrummed at his wrists and throat.

The wind soothed him slightly. He would have to trust her to devise a life for herself. He would have to learn how to leave things to time. The professor looked up at the black sky and the streaks of silver lined clouds.

He was startled out of his wits by an enormous owl that alighted somewhere above him, after flying low over the fields and vineyards between his house and the distant Villa Marnisi.

*

Fifteen

Falling masonry

The Australian doctor's surprise at his wife's willingness to listen to his dream of a small guest house in Malta was a pleasant one. He put down the phone in happy puzzlement. Could Meg be humouring him, and going along with this recitation of hopeful plans, of dreamy speculation, just to let him have a hypothetical dream and be done with it? Perhaps his wild ideas were just that – wild.

There was a moment when she said, 'Philip – you're a *doctor*.' It was the moment he realized he might not miss practising if he just stopped. He might not miss the clinic, or the surgery, or the doctors with whom he shared the general practice. What would they think?

He knew it would only put them out temporarily, for a week or two, and they would take another doctor on and resume, almost as if nothing had happened. He remembered how it went when the oldest GP in the practice, Carl Economus, retired, almost without notice, about three years ago. They feted him, had two farewell parties, bought him a ridiculously expensive gift, an enormous card signed all over with good wishes, and that was about it. He was gone and his replacement became part of the furniture inside six months. It was like water rushing in to fill a void, leaving nothing noticeable when it settled and gurgled into place.

'I know I'm a doctor,' he said, half to Meg and half to himself. 'But the thought of giving everything up and running a small bed and breakfast in the Mediterranean sounds like semi-retirement – of the most attractive kind.' He expected her to snap at him, to bite off the end of his sentence.

There was silence on the line for a long instant.

She spoke unusually slowly. 'I know it could go horribly wrong. I know you could lose a lot of money, and waste years of your time. Besides – isn't the place a *ruin*?' Meg's practicality came to the fore.

Why did he only notice she stressed her last words when they spoke on the phone? He opened his mouth to say something.

She hadn't finished. 'But, Philip ... but ... I have done some thinking. How ...?'

'It would take four or five months to put everything right. The asking price is ridiculously affordable. And it includes all the land. We could ...' dreams built it all in his mind's eye. 'We could build cottages, or host weddings ... it's all possible.'

'Philip ...'

'Look, Meg ...'

He did not speak in the pause. He could imagine her eyes slitting while she thought. What *was* she thinking?

'How about I hop on a plane and ... hm ... just for a week.'

'Or two.'

She laughed.

It was the kind of laugh Philip could never decipher.

'You twisted my arm.'

'What?'

'I'll do it. I'll come and spend a couple of weeks with you in Malta, Philip.'

He still could not figure out why his wife was being so positive.

It took Meg ten days to arrange and organize everything. He met her at Luqa airport in the heaviest rainfall he had experienced anywhere.

'Goodness – a deluge.'

'Well, it's been dry as dust for ages. I'm glad you brought some weather with you.' It was good to see her. All the tension between them seemed to have evaporated with time and distance. Philip hoped it would not return. 'What do you want to see first?'

She laughed. 'The other side of eight hours' sleep. It was a rotten flight. I'd forgotten how long it takes. Twenty-one hours! This is the end of the *earth*.'

Philip shook his head, thinking it might be the other way around, but said nothing.

They did little for Meg's first two days on the island but revisit places they had seen on their honeymoon; a kind of pilgrimage.

'It's changed so much! Those funny buses are gone.'

'Yes. Everything's changed, but the countryside is peaceful, and the distant villages still have that special feel about them.'

They drove to Żejtun and had lunch in a cellar wine bar whose walls Philip pointed out. 'Limestone, see? Thick limestone – the whole island is made of it, and they hew it out in large blocks and build incredibly beautiful houses. Many of them are lying abandoned. Too many. Just like ... do you feel like driving down the road to Villa Sans Souci?' He hoped she would say yes.

'Why not, Philip. You've been dying to show me since I got here. I hardly remember the place.'

'We must come back here, though. This lunch was rather good.'

'Yes – I thought it'd be a breathless affair, eating down in a cellar, but it's *good*.'

A waitress saw them up the stairs and out. 'There are some very old cellars around this part of the island, hewn right into the bedrock.' She seemed to know her stuff. 'I'm an archaeology student.' She gave a brilliant white smile. 'I only wait on tables part time, to pay for a new car.'

'So what do you know about the old houses around here?'

'A few were built over basic village dwellings,

which had cellars already excavated, so the steps are ancient, some predating even the ancient wayside chapels of the area.'

'Really!'

'And some cellars were used as air-raid shelters during World War Two. A few were enlarged and connected with additional tunnelling, and families would share shelters. There was a public one too, somewhere in Marsaxlokk, but I can't remember exactly where.'

They drove down the Żejtun road with rain threatening to pour again.

'Look – there's someone outside.'

Meg could not see. 'Where?'

'It's Tony.' Philip could not hold back a smile.

She turned to look at the side of his face. 'You've made local friends, already – that's not like you.'

Philip shrugged. 'Not a friend, exactly. The local busybody. Let's see what he has to say.' He pulled up on the loose gravel strip and hailed the man, who stood arms akimbo, wearing huge sunglasses dotted with raindrops, and an irrepressible smile.

'I thought you were going to roll up with ... you know ...' He looked at Meg. '... someone else.'

Meg turned to look at Philip with a blank look on her face.

Philip had to laugh. 'Who do you mean, exactly, Tony?'

'Well – he was here looking for you. Gave me a card. Stood in the sun forever, talking, talking, talking. Saying you would know about some *amount* or other.'

'*He?* Do you mean Charl Emmaus?' He took the card from Tony, while introducing him to Meg. 'This is my wife Meg.'

She smiled and said hello, watching Philip silently all the while.

The doctor looked at the card, identical to the one given to him at the restaurant. 'Yeah – Charl Emmaus. What was she doing here?' He did remember she had said she would be there one of those days.

'*She?*'

Meg looked from her husband to the Maltese man and back. 'How could it be? Same name, different person?'

'This is an unusual name, Meg. There can't be two people called Charl Emmaus – not even on an island like Malta, where everyone's got the same seven last names.'

Tony laughed. '*Seven!* Ha ha ha. Borg, Cassar, Spiteri, Mercieca, Tabone ... ha ha! Camilleri, Debono, Sant ... *Eight* Ha ha! Vella – *nine!*'

They all laughed. It was impossible to keep a straight face when Tony bellowed his laughter.

'Are you sure it was a man?'

'Look – the truth? I know him. We all know him. He hangs around down by the restaurants near the wharf down there, selling cruises and car hire and cheap flights and things.'

Philip shaded his eyes from the watery sun and looked at Meg. 'Amazing. And yet when I was being pitched the sale of this house, it was a woman ... high heels, dangling earrings, bright red lipstick and all.'

'A transvestite?' Meg was perplexed.

Philip remembered the perfect make-up, the extraordinarily high heels, the straight up-and-down figure.

Tony did not give Charl Emmaus too much deep thought. 'A trans-something, anyway! Ha ha! Definitely a commission agent. And if she ... or he ... found you a good price for the house, Philip ...' Tony gave a less than subtle wink to Meg, raising his eyebrows dramatically. '... perhaps you should consider it.' He rubbed finger and thumb together under his nose.

'This would make a nice bed and breakfast place,' Philip had to admit.

'It's been tried before, as you know.' He waved a

hand at the house. 'Not a lasting success.'

'Hm.' The doctor turned to look at the crumbling façade. He was not as certain or persuaded as he was before Meg's arrival. Seeing it through her eyes, the realization it would take several hundred thousand to make it habitable hit his realism muscle, as Meg would say.

But she was already ahead of the men, trying to find a way in. 'Someone said there might be a cellar. A really old one.'

'Did they mention the treasure, too? Ha ha!'

Philip remembered the mention of a 'treasure' at Jessie's haberdashery shop. 'Buying a property, and then finding a treasure, is the stuff dreams are made of.'

'Or nightmares. You'd have to get past the *ħares* that guards it, first.'

'The what?'

Philip explained what the word meant to his wife, watching her sceptical expression with unrevealed mirth. Any minute now, she would start to have fun. 'So this is the kind of ghost that guards a treasure. It's not a *fatat,* that lives on a staircase and frightens people away.'

'Let's have a look – I'm sure we can find a cellar if we look.' Enthusiasm was written all over Meg's face.

Philip knew it would only last until she got a whiff of the stink at the bottom of the winding staircase, if they ventured there again.

'Coming, Tony?'

'Not today, sorry. It's going to rain, really hard. It's going to pour. Have fun exploring. And good luck with the purchase!'

Philip held up a hand. 'Oh, we're not sure at all that... we haven't decided anything ...'

But the man was gone, vaulting the front heap of rubble like a man half his age.

And she was off too, ahead of him, looking

down, around and up at the sky through the height of three storeys with no floors, ceilings, or roof. 'Goodness!' Her voice rebounded off the streaked walls. 'When it rains, it must be awfully wet in here.'

Philip held back. Something held him back. He watched his wife from the distance of the ruined hallway. She might soon call to announce she had found the low doorway in what used to be the kitchen. He turned and looked up, eyes seeking the mural. A slant of light got in his eyes and it was invisible, but suddenly appeared when he took a step backwards. There it was, fresh as the day it was painted.

A rustle was in his ears. The rustle of silk, or taffeta, or something whose scent was in his head. Sandalwood, and a hint of incense.

'I cannot believe you have returned. Your audacity is remarkable.'

Philip whirled on the spot, startled, the hair on the back of his neck raised, his skin crawling with fright. 'Who's there?'

'Don't look up! Who do you think you are? This is intolerable, a return to a house from which you were so summarily dismissed. A *ħuttab*, in my house? How dare you!'

He knew what the word meant. She thought he was a marriage broker, a matchmaker, come to pose a conjugal offer. He knew his suit was not fine enough, that his shoes needed resoling, and that his bowtie was not perfectly knotted. *Tie it perfectly, and it will stay perfect*, he heard a female voice say in his head. He shrank from that voice.

'I'm not a matchmaker,' he said, afraid to raise his voice. A chilly draught caught him in the neck. He croaked, his voice became weak. Still, it rebounded around him, echoed by the perfect marble on the glimmering floors, the curved wrought-iron railing of the banister, the gleaming chandelier suspended in the middle of the stairwell.

'You formed a misguided arrangement with my

father. An imprudent plan. Well – he has apologized, and we are reconciled. We have consigned the whole ugly episode to the past. You risk ruining everything by coming back. What could you want? What could you *want?*'

'I have never met your father.' A protestation of that nature might not work, he thought. Even approaching the first step might not be a good idea; but his feet moved forward of their own accord. He was halfway up the stairs; he moved closer to her. The air was sharp and his spine felt numb and rigid with cold. His stomach shrank.

'You are after his collection, is that it? In that case, the bell will be rung, to summon help from all over the district. Your plans are dust, sir.' Her voice was as cold as the air around her.

He took in her costume of striped grey material, the perfectly straight hem of the skirt, which showed a glimpse of shiny black button-down shoes. He ascended another three stairs.

'I'm not interested in any collection.'

'You lie!' Her loud cry came with one peal from a bell, from somewhere above their heads.

He recognized the melancholic, forbidding clang. 'Oh god.'

'You may well summon your god, but no one and nothing can help you now.'

He had to think of a way to appease her. 'What can I do to ... to make amends?'

She took a step forward, and they were level, but distant. Closer, but at such a remove as to make her appearance suddenly unclear.

Philip rubbed his eyes like a child.

'Do not attempt to trespass on my lands, my belongings, my *time*. Do you understand? This is my time, and I shall protect it with everything I have.'

Philip nodded.

Her skirt rustled. There was a slight jingle from two keys that hung from a chain at her waist. 'My father's things are safe. He is very unwell. The last thing he needs is to hear an argument on the stairs from an unwelcome visitor.'

Behind her, the mural took on a greenish appearance, as if it became overgrown with a slimy mould. Philip took a step back and slipped on something viscous. His stomach turned, despite the freezing grip the conversation had cast it in.

'Someone will see you out.' She turned to face the mural, and her grey outfit seemed to melt into it; into the trellises and the foliage hanging from them, into the distant yellowing landscape of low flat-roofed buildings and church belltowers. Into the deep blue of distant Marsaxlokk Bay.

The bell sounded once again; one low toll that chilled Philip. What note was it? Why did it strike such a feeling of dread into his chest? Turning on the slippery marble stair was dangerous. It was treacherous underfoot. He grabbed the air while falling backward, slamming onto his back, which robbed him of all his breath at once. 'Oooof!'

Somewhere in the back of the house, he heard Meg's voice. Was she talking to someone? He dusted himself down and turned towards the sound of her voice.

'Philip!'

He found her just inside the doorway Tony had cleared of rubble when they were there together.

'It's not exactly clean in here. It stinks. But there's a doorway ...'

'Yes – there's a winding staircase beyond it, which goes all the way up to the roof. When there *was* a roof. It's the only really solid section of masonry in this part of the house.'

'Wow.' She started to move towards it. 'Have you been ...?'

There was a low rumbling sound.

'Thunder. Tony was right.'

It was not thunder. The ominous sound was

displacement of rolling and falling blocks of stone, and Meg screamed once. A cloud of limestone dust rose and Philip could not see clearly, but Meg had fallen through something, because he could not see her any longer. She was gone, swallowed by the bottom of the winding staircase.

'Meg!'

She did not answer. Another rumble of falling stone, and another cloud of dust and dirt rose around Philip. 'Meg!

The pile of stone at the bottom of the *garigor*, over which Tony had clambered so easily some days ago, was gone, leaving a cavity so large, so deep, that Meg disappeared into it.

'Meg! Are you all right?' He shouted into the hollow, pushing back large pieces of broken stone blocks. Debris clinked, scraped, and cracked all around him. There at his feet was a mess of dust and limestone fragments, which had blocked the way before. At Philip's feet a rectangular cavity gaped, which had been hidden by two or three *xorok*, those roofing slabs of limestone whose use someone had explained, of the same kind that still held up part of the landing in front of the mural.

He peered into the void. There was a niche, a cavity in the wall immediately below the opening; one of those stairway cupboards Tony called a *gabinett*. Most of the fragments and dust had fallen into it. And lower down, more triangular winding steps led into the darkness. 'Meg!'

He noted the central limestone handrail, the treads of the steps. They were yellow and looked comparatively unused. They looked as if they had been recently oiled or varnished, or sealed in some way, but it could be that they had not seen much use. The spiral trumpeted, funnelled and flattened the sound of his voice. 'Meg!'

And hers. 'Philip! I found it.'

'God! Where are you?' Gratitude that she

sounded all right flooded in. Relief made his knees weak and he sighed a breath so deep it dizzied him. 'Where are you?'

'There's only one way to come, Philip – down. Come on! Come *down*.'

He stepped over rubble and dust, and descended the funny triangular steps, spiralling downward into darkness. It felt gradually cooler all the way down, gradually becoming quite cold and damp. It was like sinking into a well. He counted. Like a child he counted the steps. Seventeen to the bottom.

She was in darkness, smiling, shining the light from her mobile phone into a corner.

'Are you hurt? That's quite a drop. You must have fallen ... what? Ten feet?'

'No ... no – I landed on my feet on the third or fourth step. Nothing to it! Just a bit of a fright, that's all.' She giggled.

'It smells down here. It smells funny. Golly gosh – it's ... enormous.' The room was large and felt cavernous and unusual. 'It's dug out of the bedrock, like that waitress said.'

'Yes, chipped, chiselled, with a pickaxe or stone axe. By hand – goodness! It must have taken ages.'

'But look what's here, Meg – this place is undisturbed. No one's been down here ... not recently, at any rate.'

There was a large sideboard or dresser, covered in the recent dust they disturbed themselves. One of its lower doors hung half open, and they could see folded linens inside.

'Let's not touch anything.'

'Mm – you're right. This place isn't ours, Meg.'

'*Yet*. It's becoming more interesting by the minute.'

Philip laughed and it felt eerie in the underground place. 'We're going to have to go back for a torch. Two torches.'

'Let's just have a look, a little look first. When do

you think this place was last used ... or entered, even?'

'No idea. Look – a few old books.' He looked at the spines. 'Italian, I think.'

'Or Maltese – do you know what Maltese looks like when it's written?'

'Yes – it's a profusion of exes, aitches, zeds ... they cut through some of the aitches, and some letters have a dot over them. It's unlike any other language.'

They could hardly see each other in the gloom.

'It smells musty, and my light's faltering.'

'Let's come back with torches.'

She moved away from him. 'Look. Look – this doorway ... it leads away. It's ... oh, look. There's another room in there.'

Philip turned and looked upward through the spiral of the staircase they had descended. 'Let's come back tomorrow.' He didn't like the idea of more masonry falling and blocking their way out.

There was a rumbling sound, this time real thunder, followed almost immediately by a sharp crackle of lightening, audible above their heads. 'Let's go, Meg. One of the things that eroded this place to a ruin was weather like this.'

'I want to explore. This is so exciting.' She turned to him. 'Philip, you know – we can start something here. I loved that cellar wine bar today.'

'Meg ...'

'No, listen. Can you see this place all done up, using ... you know, local materials? We could have our bed and breakfast, but we could also have a little cellar bar or wine shop or bistro or something. Look – it's huge!'

'Meg ...'

'We could run lights and things into the niches ... oh! It would be quite amazing.'

'It would cost a bomb to do up.'

She laughed. 'Right now I want to explore that other room. Let's see how big it is ... just let's look at its size, please, Philip.'

They paced through a short tunnel, which was coved about a foot from their heads. It led further downward. 'Do you know what these are? We're walking on ancient steps – more ancient than a wayside chapel – do you remember what that girl said?'

'Yes, but ...'

'Ancient, Philip!'

They emerged into a larger space, which was somehow not as dark as the previous room.

Light, and the spattering of rain water, which dropped and splashed into a puddle already there, streamed in from a shaft aperture at the far end.

'Is that a window?'

'It couldn't be.'

It was a barred shaft, unglazed, its construction laden with years of dead vegetation, soil, litter and compressed dirt. They stood underneath and looked at its sloping sides. 'So out there, up there, past that muck, is the garden, or something.'

'Yes, it's a true cellar, Meg. And that out there is a gathering storm.'

'Do you want this place? I really want this place.' Her eyes shone in a ray of grey ominous light from the garden of Villa Sans Souci.

*

Sixteen

A wall niche

The professor lay in the middle of his wide bed, propped up on large pillows which had just been changed. His papery eyelids quivered, and his lips seemed to mumble something like poetry.

Certainly not prayer. Not prayer. My father does not pray. She was tired, but watched her father closely through her white veil. His temperature had started to improve earlier in the evening.

'It goes down. The temperature of people that sick, that infirm, generally goes down slightly at sunset. I still don't understand why he had a high temperature at all. It's unusual.' The nurse nodded sagely, declaring her experience calmly. She wore her cap too low on her forehead, and her stockings were wrinkled at the ankles. She had draped her cape over the back of a chair without folding it. She moved to a side table and tightened the cap of a small blue bottle, read its label once more, and nodded again.

She ventured a look toward Prasseide. 'There is no ... In this room ... over the bed. You have no ...?'

The doctor's daughter let her talk on. She did not speak in the nurse's pauses, allowing the older woman's embarrassment to grow.

'Perhaps you might like to bring in a comforting image. Or statue? Or a crucifix.'

'Oh. Is that what you mean? There is no sacred art in our house, nurse. You will find no holy pictures, or icons, or crucifixes.'

The nurse gasped. 'But I thought ...'

'Let's not do too much thinking. I am sure you come prepared, for yourself, with some medal around your neck, or rosary beads in your pocket. You needn't worry about my father's comfort ... other than his physical wellbeing. It's good that you have seen to the changing of his linen.'

'But he whispers prayers.'

'I am sure he does not.'

Prasseide went out on the landing and closed the double doors of the bedroom behind her, then pushed them open a crack and saw how the nurse leaned close to the doctor, trying to catch words. Yes, they were words, but not in any language she understood. She thought this was a strange household, and it was quite likely she wished Doctor Buhagiar in Żejtun had chosen someone else for this vigil. The afternoon's conversation chilled her. Prasseide could see her discomfort plainly through the veil close to her face. Each word was etched in her mind.

'Your father is very ill, I'm afraid.'

'It's why you are here, nurse.'

'Doctor Buhagiar has now ordered double doses of the specially compounded medicine.'

Prasseide looked at the blue bottle and a round brown box made of compressed paper, whose circular label was scrawled illegibly. 'I'm sure he knows best.'

'This is strong medicine. It would kill a mule if taken all at once.'

The veil moved to the rhythm of her breathing. She paused before she spoke again. 'I hardly think it is likely a mule could get at this medicine, nurse.'

'Your father will ... would ... go ... if we didn't have such strong medicines.'

'When my father goes, nurse, I shall go with him.'

The nurse looked startled. 'How do you know? No one knows when they will be called.'

'Called or not ... what did you say about a mule?' She had seen a mule, very recently. It was led up the Żejtun road by a small boy. He waved a sprig of some sort of shrub about its head, both to keep the flies out of its eyes, and to urge it forward. She saw the boy push the mule to the side of the road, close up against the rubble wall, when a woman came the other way driving a small herd of goats. She was on her way to sell milk in Żejtun, in the freshest way possible; straight from the goat. People would come to their front doors with all manner of receptacle, and the goats were milked into clay pot, china cup, tin saucepan, enamel bowl, porcelain jug.

But the boy with the mule was a curious sight on that road. She had never seen beasts of burden without a rough saddle, or harnessed into a small wooden cart, or perhaps wearing a rope halter of some sort. This child simply pushed the animal along, spoke to it, and waved that branch in a kind of semaphore, which the beast seemed to understand.

'Ejja, ejja!' He shouted in a shrill voice, clicked his tongue in the side of his mouth, and they were off down the road. She watched them until they were out of sight, the boy in his threadbare cut-down man's trousers, and the mule with its floppy ears and uneven gait.

She wondered what it would take to kill a beast that size; standing in the semi-darkness of her father's sick room. She moved to a chair and perched lightly on it, craning her neck to see if her father's lips still trembled. Then she heard the words.

'Marianna. Bring Marianna to my side. I wait for Marianna.' He repeated his dead wife's name over and over. 'Marianna. Do not leave me in the dark, I beg you. Light a lamp. Two lamps. *Għall-erwieħ.*'

It affected Prasseide, and her eyes filled with tears. If only those double doors would open now, and let her mother into the room. She would glide in as she used to, with those wide gathered skirts. She would lean forward elegantly, from the waist, take her husband's hand, and comfort him. She would turn her head sideways and look at Prasseide with her beautiful eyes that were shrouded with sorrow, and say she would sing to them, to them both. And everything would immediately be better.

And her voice would sound in the room, and float outward, and reverberate near the mural, and descend the great stairway, and live forever in the hall.

'Oh, I do so much wish Mama would come in and sing you a song.' She moved close and took his hand. 'Papa? Do you hear? I will call her to sing you a song.' She leaned close to his mouth.

'Marianna. Marianna.' His breathing was laboured, and a visible pulse ticked at his temple. 'Light a lamp. It's so dark.'

Prasseide left his bedside, went to the dressing table, where she remembered her mother sitting and brushing her hair, or dusting scented powder on her skin, or taking the crystal knob off a bottle of sandalwood scent, and dabbing the stopper behind her ears. Prasseide raised her veil, leaned toward the mirror, and looked at her ravaged face. She gazed into her own eyes, squinted, opened them wide. 'Come and sing a song, Mama.' *If only. If only.* 'Come, Mama, come!'

The room filled with the sound of a beautiful voice in full song. It was only a few seconds, but it was melodious, strong, and it set the curtains trembling. Prasseide replaced her veil.

'I heard you singing.' The nurse entered and closed the door quietly behind her. 'And you have lit the lamps!'

'That was Mama.' She left in a swirl, her taffeta skirt rustling.

'But ...' The nurse was more confused than ever.

Prasseide popped her veiled face around the door. 'I'm going to ask the coachman and his sons to bring my harp down – I shall play softly to my father, while he dies.'

'While he ...' The nurse had never met anyone who spoke so plainly about death. She felt much better when she was alone in the room with the sick man. But she had to stand back, hardly half an hour after the daughter spoke her words, for two men to gently lower a large gilt harp to the carpet in the corner of the doctor's bedroom.

'You ... um ... you won't play now?'

'Later, nurse.'

'We should really get some air. Perhaps the downstairs maid – is her name Rosa? – can sit with the doctor for ten minutes. Would you walk with me on the road outside? They said one can see the sea if one walks far enough.'

'If one walks far enough, one can walk *into* the sea. This is the road between Żejtun and Marsaxlokk. It's an important thoroughfare. And no, I shall not walk with you. You may take a walk in the garden, to the gazebo and back. If you climb the five steps to the gazebo, you can see the sea.'

'Oh, how wonderful.'

'I shall sit with my father. Please go. Get some air.'

When she returned, the nurse would find her arranging flowers in the shallow wall niche between the bedroom windows. Prasseide laughed to herself, knowing she would be puzzled, knowing the older woman's consternation would be unbearable if she watched her light votive candles and place them behind a large ivory carving, whose piercings allowed light through, so her father might see it from the bed.

Prasseide did not turn when she heard the double doors open and shut again. She continued, lighting another candle, fixing daisies and lilies so they formed a pleasing arrangement, angling the carving so that candlelight came through its apertures, slits and perforations, throwing dancing motes of light on the patterned tiles of the floor.

*

Seventeen

Bell arch

Philip saw it was time he confided in his wife. She was sitting on the sea wall, happily licking an ice cream cone, unaware of his state of mind. The house and its shadowy occupants, its history and atmosphere, had got under his skin.

He pocketed change in light unfamiliar coins, thinking they might become very familiar if he stayed on the island much longer. When he paced toward his wife, he wished she sat further away, so his thoughts would take time to settle, to hit upon a way to let her know how he was affected by the whole Villa Sans Souci business. It was a difficult thing to get his head around. He was torn between a number of things, but could not clearly identify them. What was it that was really bothering him – that was really essential to solve?

He wanted to explain himself, he wanted to talk about the house and what he saw, but did not want to frighten her off, or get her to think him insane. He had no medical explanation why his blood ran cold, or why he sometimes lost hours without being able to explain what happened.

She would think him mad. All he could think of, now, was the strange shift in her behaviour. She was patient and sweet; nothing like the Meg he had stormed away from when he took that plane to Malta. She was so bitter when he left.

When a woman said, *I've changed and you haven't noticed* ... that was the time for a man to have a good long look at himself and how he treated the relationship. Philip had counselled many patients about this. Could he look at his own life in an objective way? He doubted it. This was no time to get cocky and overly self-assured. But there was no real alternative to talking about it. And Meg seemed to be well disposed now. Now. What brought on the positive change? He doubted if he would ever find out.

He looked at her against the background of the bay. Marsaxlokk was a pretty place. And the colourful fishing boats, what the brochures and websites spoke about, were only one of the attractive aspects of the place. It was different. Sliema and St Julians had nothing on this. He knew because a visit to the resort towns had giddied and dismayed him; they were little more than tourist appeasers. Souvenirs, cheap food, standard harbour cruises, standard historic tours, all touted by multi-lingual commission sellers and guides ... it was not the kind of place he sought. This was his idea of a better place to spend a holiday.

Was this a holiday? He approached Meg deciding it was, but it was also something else. Something they needed to talk about.

'Let's go back to that wine cellar place for lunch.' She spoke when he was still several yards away. She looked young, like the Meg he had brought here on honeymoon, before he knew how general practice would affect him, before they had the children, before providing for their retirement even entered their heads.

He took her back to Żejtun, where they wandered to the end of the village and found the chapel dedicated to Saint Clement.

'Philip – look at the bell arch. It's just like the one ... like the ruined one on top of our villa!'

'*Our* villa!'

'You know what I mean. Villa Sans Souci. Wouldn't it be spectacular if it was restored, and a bell hung there once more?'

'Yes, um ... spectacular. Look, Meg, you must have noticed I'm surprised at your new enthusiasm about this place. There's stuff I need to talk to you about.'

'I hope it doesn't have anything to do with a transgender woman called Charl.' She pulled her face into a funny grimace.

Relieved she was full of humour, Philip led the way towards the wine bar cellar where they would enjoy another platter of local produce and some excellent wine.

'There's something funny about that house, Meg. I've *seen* things.'

'What things?'

'I'm not sure. Visions. The mural – sometimes it's as fresh as the day it was done. I got paint on my fingers, from the foliage.'

She laughed, but he could see she wanted to hear more. 'When? When did you get paint on your fingers from a mural painted a hundred years ago?'

'The first time. On our honeymoon. Twenty-five years ago.'

'And ...'

'And?'

'And a woman.' He tried to find words to describe what he saw. 'A ... I'm not sure if I saw her or just felt she was there. I ...'

'I knew there was a woman in there somewhere.'

'What? You saw her too ...?'

'No.' Meg stopped on the road and turned to look him in the eye, whipping off her sunglasses and shading her eyes with a capped hand. 'No – I mean I knew there was some woman in your story. You've been acting strangely, and when that happens ...'

He saw her reasoning. 'Goodness, Meg – there's no one else. I mean I see ... I feel the presence of this veiled woman, in the house. Not very nice.'

'You're just burnt out. You've put too much of yourself into the practice. You haven't come up for breath for years. The kids and I have just waited and waited.'

'I know.'

'No – you don't. You have no idea how ...'

'So why did you come out to join me and ... why this holiday? You're being so wonderful. And understanding. And enthusiastic. More enthusiastic than me about the house!'

She took a deep breath and looked along the road, now full of traffic, which would take them through to the wine bar. 'Let's walk. I'll tell you why – it's because you're sounding so rested. This house seems to be a blessing ...'

'Not a curse?' Sometimes it felt cursed to him.

'No. Just think. The kids are now so independent. It happened so quickly. So what if we abandon your practice and all that, and come and spend a few years running a bed and breakfast here?'

'See? That's what I mean. What's motivated you, Meg? Why do you want to do this all of a sudden?'

She shook her head. 'How do I know? I want to see you well and happy. I want a change ... a good change for once. I want some adventure, I suppose.'

'Adventure.' He thought of being accosted on the stairs of that house – stairs that no longer existed – by a vision that sent him toppling backwards onto a pile of debris. That could be called an adventure. 'I want you to listen to what I've seen, Meg.'

She listened, while he told her some of it. They ate salads and small local cheeses, olives grown in nearby groves and seasoned with fresh herbs and garlic, and drank some delicious white wine.

Meg listened to everything he said.

'So you think there's a hidden treasure, or something.'

'No! No, Meg. I just feel I've stumbled on the local ghost, The White Lady, and she's chosen me, of all people, to ... to ... look – I don't know.'

'To put her to rest? To stop her having to reappear?'

Did Meg understand at last? 'Could it be that?' Philip put down his glass and looked at the bare limestone walls of the cellar restaurant. 'It could be. Why didn't I think of that?' He stopped to think. 'But how can I ... Am I crazy?'

'This is different, that's for sure.' Meg sat back. 'At first I thought it was all a big excuse. A cover-up for something you wanted to keep from me.'

'What – like another woman?'

She nodded.

'I hardly had time for *you*.'

'I know.' Her face was hard.

'Look, I'm sorry.' He did not know what else to say. 'At the same time, I feel there's something here I can't ignore.'

'I see that. You need to lay this ghost, Philip.'

'Seriously?' Did she believe anything he said? The white veil? The pocked face? The rustling fabric and paint on his fingers? Looking down at his legs and seeing serge trousers and leather boots? Seeing marble and chandeliers, banisters and stairs that were not there?

She took her napkin and pleated it slowly, contemplatively, making an accordion pattern out of the folds, silent and pensive.

Philip let her think.

'Is this about the house, Philip? Or is it about us?' At last she asked the right questions, in a soft voice.

He did not know the answer. 'What do you think?'

'Both, I think. I think the opportunity to change everything is really exciting. I also feel a bit guilty.'

'You? What's happened? What have you done?'

'Something really stupid.'

Philip Falzon's heart sank. It would serve him right if Meg had strayed, or if she had set her heart on something and spent a lot of money. Or if she had decided to go her own way at some point. He did not know what to say. 'Stupid?'

'I blamed you for everything. I was pretty resentful of the practice getting more attention than us, I hardly said goodbye when you took off – *stay there in that rotten house*, I thought ... but you're not a bad man, Philip. I regretted it, after you phoned.'

'So that's why so came so willingly.'

She smiled. 'Mm. I had lots of time to think, see? We could change tack and do something different, you know ... we could make it work. But we could also ruin everything we've worked so hard to build. It won't break the bank to buy that place and restore it ... I really want to. Part of me really wants to.'

'Me too.'

'And part of me is cautious enough, still, to say *Hey! Watch what you're doing*. We could just be taking our problems and ... and exporting them to Malta.'

'Hm. What's at stake here?' Philip decided to try and reason out the dilemma with a set of strategic principles applied at work. Would it work? 'We could lose some money. We could burn up some time.'

'But we could have fun, fix our relationship, and start semi-retirement, couldn't we?'

'There would be so many problems.'

'Most of them external to you and me. External to us. We need that kind of problem. Like when we were struggling, like when the children were babies and we were both pitted against the world. Together. See what I mean?' She smiled and nodded at the waiter, who asked if everything was fine. 'It's wonderful, thank you. We love this place.' She paused.

'Meg – '

She put a hand on his arm. 'Look, Philip – we've had problems before, we've worked hard before. Nothing new. It's just that this is really different. Different place. Different people.'

Different time. His mind rang with the words. *Different time.* He said them. 'Different time.'

Meg laughed. She understood what he meant. 'We'll just have to lay your ghost.'

'Perhaps I won't feel or see or smell anything again, simply because I've told someone about it.'

'You said the whole town thinks the place is haunted.'

'The whole country.'

'Has anyone else seen her?'

'We should ask Tony. Tony's the best bet, because we surely won't get much that's true from Charl Emmaus.'

'I'd love to meet her.'

'Really? Quite a forceful character.'

*

Eighteen

The glass door to the terrace

The professor died on a bright sunny afternoon, in the all-encompassing sound of crickets singing their continual joyous racket outside his windows. His nurse was absent, taking a break down in the side garden, climbing up and down the gazebo steps, gazing out at the line of blue that was the sea, walking toward the house and looking up at the tall house wall, one section of which was perforated by a vertical line of six small unglazed windows, shaped like little shields. She knew they let air and light into the *garigor*, up and down which she had climbed so often during her brief stay at this villa.

The doctor died, with his daughter by his side. She held his hand and watched him take his last breath. She was calm, with grief that did not display itself, for now, in tears or loud cries of sorrow.

'Farewell, Papa.' She said the words under her breath, and did not lean back in the bedside chair, but stayed attentive and vigilant over his still form. She did not rise to call the nurse. She would come eventually, that untidy woman with wrinkled stockings. She would open the double bedroom doors and find her still sitting there, holding her dead father's hand.

No, no. She would arrive from her break and find her playing the harp, softly and slowly. The Beethoven songs of Switzerland; melodies from when she was but a child. But first, she needed to clear away the evidence of his long illness. She hid the medicines, the folded towels, the tray of sad necessities.

'That's better.' Her mind raced and slowed, filled with thought and then emptied, time after time. What would become of her? What would happen to the house? Where would she end her days? Her fingers travelled on the strings of the harp, back and forth, plucking and tugging. Music filled the room.

Gradually, the light shifted, and a ray of sunlight rested on the dressing table, where once her mother's brushes and scent bottles stood. She knew where they were. She knew where they kept things that were no longer in use. Her father's fountain pen, his signet ring, the cases of ivory artefacts ... would they too be consigned down, down, downward in the house to the darkness of the cellar store, where they would be wrapped in tissue, and then in linen, until ... until what?

Her fingers played and played.

The nurse's entry disturbed Prasseide's thoughts. 'I am back.' She was out of breath from inhaling fresh air and hurrying up the spiral staircase at the back of the house. 'I heard the music.'

'Was there a sea breeze?' Prasseide stopped playing and stood.

'Yes, quite fresh. But the sun is sharp and strong. It's quite ...' The nurse stopped. She saw the doctor's still, pale visage. She noted the lack of rise and fall of his chest. She heard the quiet of the afternoon. The crickets had stopped, the light had travelled across the room and was now almost spent. 'Oh, miss ...'

'*Sinjura*. You must address me as *sinjura*. I am the mistress of the house. Now more than ever.'

'You did not call for me. I was so close. You played ...'

Prasseide turned to face her. 'I could have walked across the landing, opened the glass door to the terrace, stood out there and called, over the garden. *My father is dead,* I could have called.'

The nurse gasped.

'I did not even go out on the landing to look at the mural.'

'The mural.' The older woman was reduced by her surprise to repeating what Prasseide said.

'He had it painted so that we would have that beautiful view inside and out.'

'And out.'

'Please make all the arrangements for my father's last rites. He will also have an elegant and fitting funeral. I shall speak, I suppose, to the cousins in Valletta. Please get Karist to send for them.'

'Yes, yes. Is there no one I can send for, to sit with you during this ...?'

'This sorrowful time? No. I have always been alone. The cousins will arrive in time.' Her eyes behind the veil blinked.

If the nurse could see the hollows of the woman's eyes behind the veil she would have gasped again, this time in horror. 'Alone.'

'Yes. I shall sit in the green room. And Mama will join me.'

'Oh, *sinjura* ...' The nurse was close to tears, simply because she detected none on the bereaved daughter's face.

'Do what I said.'

Prasseide did not attend her father's funeral, because it would have reminded her too much, too sorely, of her mother's. She watched the hearse, whose six black-plumed horses clip-clopped away from the house he had had built so long ago, and said aloud to herself that she would never hear the sound of hooves on a tarred road again without feeling the devastation of an empty life. A life made empty by death.

The hearse reached the bend in the road to Żejtun and disappeared, but the sound of the horses' hooves stayed in her ears. The entire household walked behind, all dressed in black. Karist, Rosa, and the others. They would walk as far as the chapel of Saint Clement, and then turn back. The hearse, together with carriages and *karrozzini* following it in the long cortège, would proceed to the Addolorata cemetery, so very far away.

And she would never see her father again.

She turned and walked across the landing to the

green drawing room. 'It's not the same as with you, Mama.'

Sitting across from the beautiful gilt and brocade sofa, she lifted her veil and sat back. 'With you, Mama, it's different. You will rest when you no longer have to watch over me. I know that now. Papa's work is done. He can rest forever, in the knowledge and reassurance you are here for me.'

'And when will you rest, my dearest girl?'

Prasseide sat bolt upright and swallowed hard. She looked around the room, terrified. Her pretence was taking on a surreal aspect. 'What? Is that you, Mama?'

'When will you find peace, my dear Mary?'

'Only you call me Mary.' Tears threatened to brim over her distorted eyelids, the eyelids that never quite closed to block out the light.

'Only I.'

'I shall never rest. I shall not rest until this house is dust.'

'My child, a promise like that holds portent over which you might have some regret.' Her voice summoned darkness. 'You will exhaust everything, except yourself.' The curtains were still not drawn, the lamps still unlit, and the skies darkened so much it was frightening in that room. Thunder sounded in the distance. 'There is to be another great storm.'

'People still talk about the one ...'

'Just at the time this house was being built. It pushed everything before it, flooding vineyards, toppling walls. A builder was lost in the flood of water that came, rushing through the streets, from Għaxaq. The church of Saint Clement was inundated. Perhaps that is why their altar is so high.'

'Mama.'

'I survived that storm. I sang through it.'

'I have just played my harp through another.'

'Yes. You weathered it. You will endure.'

'No.'

'You have been thinking about your belongings.'

Prasseide lowered her head, and raised her hands to her pocked cheeks. 'They cannot be buried with me, like the great Egyptian princesses would command.'

'Bury them anyway.'

The doors to the green drawing room were thrown open, and a maid in black entered.

'You are not following the hearse!' Prasseide's voice was weary with fright and grief.

'We have all returned, *sinjura*. We all walked to the chapel of Saint Clement and back. I'm here to light the lamps.'

'And candles. Many candles. Find all the candelabras, and light many candles.'

The maid bowed her head in assent, but could not say another word.

'Has the nurse left this house?'

The maid nodded again.

'Good. When all the candles and lamps are lit, summon Karist. I have instructions for him.'

He was still in his new funeral suit, and looked awkward and graceless.

'What is it, Karist? You have stood here before.'

He shook his head.

'Do you remember your father, the old coachman, Karist?'

He nodded, perplexed.

'He was true and loyal. I want you to be true and loyal too. And *obedient*.'

His eyes were still wide, with something like awe or fright. It must have been the funeral of his master.

'Listen, and observe what I am about to say. Every word. Take heed and carry out each instruction carefully.' Then she saw what caused his nervousness. He had never seen her without a veil, and her distorted and ravaged face made him writhe with unease. His eyes were wide, appalled by her appearance.

Prasseide was silent for a full minute, in which

time the servant grew more and more uncomfortable.

Then she gave instructions about which of her father's belongings were to be stored away.

'The pens, in the tortoiseshell box, with all the gold nibs. The magnifying glass and the telescope, packed together. The books with green covers, in one crate. Those with red covers, in another. The ivory collection will fill more than one crate. Pack the good dinner service in newspaper and sawdust. Fold all the lace tablecloths between tissue. Use naphthalene. The piano in the front room is to be locked. Build a crate for the harp. The candelabras must be wrapped in linen. Take down the lace curtains.'

She went on and on, trusting he would listen attentively; would memorise everything she said, and carry out her orders. 'Fold the woollen blankets with Rosa. Strip my father's bed. Do not cover the mirrors. Empty and wrap the decanters. They go into a crate with the crystal glasses.'

For twelve days, Prasseide stayed in the green drawing room. To the discomfort of the servants and consternation of the cousin who had arrived from Valletta to stay with her, she would not move from there except to visit a water closet *gabinett* in the back stairs. Her outfit took on a worn glaze, her skin looked worse than ever, now that she stayed unveiled, and her hands shook. She ate small morsels of hard cheese and aniseed rusks. She drank scalding black coffee, unsweetened. She hardly slept, sitting upright with her head resting against the ornate back of a straight armchair. She seemed to speak to herself.

Her cousin was concerned, but did not know what to do. She sat at a discreet distance and watched her, numbly passing the time with her embroidery.

'Understand this, cousin.'

'Yes?'

'I am mourning more than just the passing of my father.'

The cousin nodded, uncomprehending.

On the thirteenth day, a slipper bath was

ordered for the fireside in her bedroom, full of warm water and drops of sandalwood oils and essences. The servants heaved sighs of relief. She ordered long sprigs of jasmine to be brought up from the garden, to be lain around her chamber.

To make sure everything had been done as she arranged, Prasseide walked around the house, opening cupboard doors, checking locks, listening to the rain that, since the night of her father's death, had not fully ceased. When the crickets ceased their noise, when her father stopped breathing, the rain came.

She sought the tray of medicinal necessities that had salved her father's pain in the last days of his life. And found it, where she had hidden it in her mother's dressing table. The blue bottle and box of compressed paper were still there, still half full. She shed her last tears.

*

Nineteen

Double colonnade

He paced on the terrace, looked out towards the sea, but everything was black at this late hour. There was no moon, and only a distant speckling of stars showed there was any sky at all. It was desolate, noiseless, forsaken and barren. Other houses in the district rang often with the laughter of children, the bleated cries of newborn babies, the groans of women in labour, the laments of farmers over late harvests, the yelped protests of young boys sent out with little herds of goats or bunches of carrots and onions to market. There were screamed quarrels among fishwives further down the road at Marsaxlokk, and the bated softened oaths of wagering men at dog fights and card games. But here, it was always silent.

He was caught here, in servitude, a coachman, gardener, valet; and even that thought brought a weight of guilt. Had he not enjoyed the tenure of his family here, where servitude was at least comfortable, accommodated in comparative comfort, furnished with requirements and comforts like no other peasant family he knew, as far away as the big palace at Verdala? He was fortunate indeed. The professor was a good employer.

Why had his lonely grief-stricken daughter asked if he remembered his old father? Of course he did. Why had she given so many strange instructions? She must be mad with anguish.

Guilt gripped his throat, and the space in his head behind his eyes. The lack of charity he felt toward her; the disgust he felt when he saw her face, were sinful. He must make penance. He had to make a pilgrimage, a journey of contemplation and atonement. He counted the number of wayside chapels he would pass if he made a walk to Verdala, that distant district he had never seen.

If he went, he would take a cane, and wrapped in a checked cloth, a loaf of bread stuffed with cheese, half a bell pepper, the hearts of two artichokes, a big ripe tomato, a fistful of boiled white beans, an onion as sweet as an apple, and enough olive oil to soak through to the crust. He would stop to give thanks at each limestone chapel. He would worship at the low grated openings, at eye level if he knelt, even if the massive wooden doors were locked. He would peer through metal bars and give thanks for having gone another mile or two.

Unable to read, he would gaze up at the plaques and coats of arms, wondering what they said, whose benefaction they depicted. He would peer in and glimpse the glimmer of an oil lamp, left to guard and light the holy presence of dark oil paintings and frescoes of saints and martyrs, donated as *ex voto* gifts, by patrons who had received favour from the chapel's saint, interceding on their behalf with the Almighty.

Now which chapel would he see first when he started off on his walk of reparation? He planned a pilgrimage of restitution, of contrition, of penance. His master was dead, and Karist felt bereft. He saw the daughter as repulsive, and had to repent. He needed to thank God, and to confess, to make amends for any shortcomings, any omissions he might have made during the doctor's life. He would walk to Verdala, he would stagger as far as the cliffs at Had-Dingli, and from there seek the mythic chantry of Simblija, which some said did not exist; or if it did, was a mere hunting lodge which once was a desecrated chapel.

It was a long walk to plan, with no means of sustenance except that received from strangers along the way. His old mother said it was madness, but he would leave her in the care of his brothers, and depart, knowing her prayers would accompany him, and that his on the way would ensure she would eventually welcome him back.

The double colonnade where he paced was majestic, tall, beautiful, but his master would never see it again. The last he saw of the doctor was his black hearse, glossy in the sunlight, pulled by six matched black horses, each bedecked with a brow set of plumes. Their harness and yokes were black as night. Their gait was contained, measured, and the top hats and veils of the coachmen matched the black festoons on their flanks.

It was a funeral cortège like no other seen in those districts since the death of the Marquesa from across the fields at Marsaskala. She was the patroness of many neighbourhood chapels, and had even founded a school, so the peasants all esteemed her, and walked behind her hearse and carriages as far as Saint Clement's, as he had done behind his master almost two weeks ago.

His heart would mend, but he doubted he could say the same for the daughter of the house, whose visage he had only seen once. Since the day of her mother's death she was morose, angry, and unapproachable. They were all scared of her sombre melancholy. Her wretchedness was of the highest order, and no one dared contradict her; even her father, when he was alive, would occasionally be numbed and struck wordless by her outbursts.

That woman could move the very limestone on which her house stood. She could chill the heart of anyone.

Karist paced the terrace. No one knew he was there. He knew the bereaved mistress was confined to the drawing room, and would not be seen for days. The cousin who was sent from Valletta to sit with her was also confined, but to rooms beyond the first locked gate on the stairs, which, since yesterday, was thrown open.

There was no longer need for that kind of

security. All the doctor's treasures were packed away and hidden below ground level. His instructions were strange, incredibly strange, and he was bidden never, ever to speak of them to anyone, so his lips were as sealed as the place where he had stored his master's things.

With them, he packed and stored also two items he never thought he would have been asked to store, but after all, he was just a servant, and would never question the orders of the mistress of the house.

She had entered her father's room, empty now; the bed stripped, his clothes removed from the enormous wardrobe, which stood open, smelling of naphthalene moth balls, revealing the fine wood of its broad interior.

'What is that?'

Karist looked to where she pointed. There was something wide and flat inside the wardrobe.

'Pull it out.'

He did what he was told and brought out a large stretched canvas, whose back had been painted brown. It was well braced, well made.

'Turn it round!'

He turned it to face her, and she gasped. She raised her hands in wretchedness and woe, and gave a subdued shriek.

'That painter! That artist! Ah. Ahhh!' Her screams rose and fell. 'Put it there ... prop it against the wall. And leave me. Leave!'

Karist left the room, closing the door softly behind him, leaving Prasseide to gaze upon the painting, the painting Lazzaro had made of her as a young girl, with perfect skin, with bright eyes, with sweet lips and a broad intelligent forehead. All in white she stood, in the green drawing room, addressing the viewer with eyes that smiled, with straight and healthy teeth, between lips that were rosy and flushed with vigour.

'So that was why he stayed so long after the

mural was done. So this is what he thinks I *should* look like. So this is what my father longed for. Ah.' She folded her arms across her chest and turned away. But she could not keep her eyes from the painting.

'Karist!' She moved to her father's bedside table and looked at the stripped bed, the mattress made of ticking stuffed with horsehair and sheep's wool. There was no way she could tell him how she felt now. In her hand, the little silver handbell shook, and rang frenzied summons.

'Karist!'

He came and stood just inside the door.

'Take this. Take the painting. Take it! Wrap it carefully in ... in sacking, in something. Wrap also my harp. Carefully! And take them down to the cellar. Place them in the niche opposite the winding stairs. Now. Go!'

She addressed him simply, but sharply, peremptorily, and since her face was now plainly visible, he did not like to gaze at her ruined features or look into those eyes. Or to tell her he had already crated the harp, or to say there were eleven crystal glasses and not a dozen.

'Crazed eyes,' he said to his mother, later that night, and instantly regretted his treachery, which he would atone on his pilgrimage to Had-Dingli, if he got that far. He would confess to a monk at San Martin, in Baħrija, and beg for bread in Rabat, near the entry to the silent city, if he found his way there. Fear struck at his heart, but it was not as strong as the fear he felt, somehow, when he first saw his mistress's face. Her eyes were something horrific, and her uneven mouth was capable, he was sure, of uttering curses.

Perhaps the sooner he left, the better. He would pray for her well-being on the way, while peering through iron bars at the altar of some chapel. He was sure she never prayed herself.

'Don't say that!' His mother had crossed herself and pulled a horned fist out of her apron pocket. 'You will bring a curse down on us all.'

Now the house was quiet. Everything might return to normal with time, but what was normal about wrapping things and hiding them in the cellar? What was normal about having fronds and branches of jasmine brought up from the garden for a bedroom? What was normal about having the slipper bath filled with warm water, when there was a perfectly good bathroom, complete with new plumbing, and a ball-and-claw footed big bath which had its own running tap, right on the same floor?

It was not his place to ask, of course. So here he was, enjoying the terrace, where it was rare for him to find himself, since it was no place for servants, especially in the dead of night. He wished for a cigarette. He had taken three from the study, and he had only one left.

And there, behind him, a female voice, loud, panicked. Ah well, it was that time, in this house; a time of sorrow and lamenting. Of crying and distress. But it was not the voice of the mistress; nor the voice of the visiting cousin.

'Karist!' It was Rosa, the faithful maid. 'Karist! *Fejn int?*' She ran up and down the big staircase, shouting his name. 'Where are you? Where are you?' Her voice was so high- pitched in distress that it was a screech, a voice full of tragedy and disaster.

'What is it, Rosa?' He pulled the shuttered doors to behind him. He hoped she would not smell his breath and discover he had been smoking. 'Keep your voice down.'

Her eyes were wide with panic and horror. 'The mistress!'

'What? What happened?'

'*Egħrqet! Egħrqet!* She drowned!'

'Rosa – please. Calm down. What happened?'

'She has drowned in the bath. She's gone. She is soaking wet. She is dead, I tell you!' Her shrieks filled the stairwell, and reverberated on the wrought-iron railing of the banister. The chandelier shook and jingled to her screams.

'Good heavens. Are you sure?'

'Come up!'

'Is it permissible? Do we need a female ...?'

'Come in – she is not ... she is *clothed*. She is clothed, in white. In the bath, soaking wet. It's terrible.'

Rosa was right. Prasseide, the professor's daughter, lay in the bath, fully submerged in the fragrant water. The pungent smell of jasmine and sandalwood was almost too intense to bear. The vision of her, in her white lace gown, which floated in wraithlike swirls around her figure in the water, was terrifying. The veil half clung to her ruined face, and her hair was starting to become unravelled from its complicated plait. Hair was plastered to her neck, and the skin of her ravaged arms was starting to pucker and become waterlogged.

'Karist! What are we to do?'

The man stood there, appalled by what he saw. The woman had climbed into the slipper bath fully dressed, down to her button-down white satin shoes. She had submerged herself under the water, and drowned. By the side of the bath was a small table, on which were an empty medicine bottle, on its side, and a compressed paper pill box. 'She has taken something. She has taken everything. She has emptied these ...'

'This room is full of sin, Karist.'

'Don't say that.' He crossed himself.

'It is a sin to end your life before God has fulfilled His plan for you.'

'Hush. Go and fetch her cousin. I cannot decide whether ...' He could not allow a lady to see this. '... good. Look – go and slowly wake up her cousin upstairs. Wait ten minutes, and then bring her down. Go!'

The maid went, and Karist locked the bedroom

door.

He approached the slipper bath and looked down upon his mistress. If he placed a hand under each of her arms, he could lift her over his shoulder and carry her to the bed.

She was very heavy. Waterlogged, saturated, squelching with sounds that terrified him, he carried her to the turned-down bed, dripping, dripping. He ruined his coachman's suit, which became soaked in the process. He drew the covers over the woman, who oozed scented water over the pillow, over the linen sheets. He adjusted the veil over her face, and moved away from the bed.

There was a light tap on the door. 'Karist? She won't come down. She is terrified.'

'It's all right. Perhaps it is for the better.' He exhaled a tortured breath. 'Perhaps it's just as well.' He strode out, pulling the door behind him. 'No one is to go in there until Doctor Buhagiar arrives from Żejtun. I shall ride to St Catherine's church for a priest.'

'Oh – yes. Yes.'

He was almost sure no priest would enter the house now. A stiff cold draught swept past him, from the door to the terrace, which he was sure he had closed, and seemed to disturb the painted foliage on the mural. The coachman shook his head and rubbed his eyes.

He strode to the drawing room and pulled a taut wire. The bell on the roof tolled. He rang it for a minute, and then stopped. 'This is a disaster, Rosa.'

'We are finished.'

'We're fine. It's the house that's doomed. No one will ever want to live here again, if word gets out. And it will.'

*

Twenty

Wiring and plumbing

She returned to the kitchen and surveyed the work that had just been done. 'Electricity and gas will make a huge difference.'

'It certainly cost enough money.'

'Don't complain, Alan. Don't complain all the time. When you're away flying your precious planes, when you're at Biggin Hill, I'll be here frying bacon and eggs, making pies and custards, and generally earning us the wherewithal to finance a decent retirement.'

'And what do you think I'm doing at Biggin Hill ... and Hal-Far... and Ta' Qali?'

She sighed and turned to look at his carefully groomed beard and moustache. He still dressed like a wartime squadron-leader. 'You wish Operation Crossbow was still on, Alan. You have no idea what to do with yourself since the end of the war. The war hasn't exactly helped our plans. You might even consider getting out of the Air Force if we get this going properly.'

He did not admit anything. Agreeing with Molly was dangerous when her attack was personal and cynical. 'Training youngsters to fly has its merits.'

'Huh!' Molly reached for a stack of white plates and carried them to a corner cupboard. 'Now let's talk about a sign.'

'A sign will make the place look cheap. We must rely on word of mouth. That's what will make this place famous.'

'Famous!' Molly was good at one-word retorts. She was also good at looks that would wilt people where they stood. She had no time for fools, and Alan was starting to feel like one.

'Molly – there's little or no hope of passing trade

here. People will come and stay if they're ... if they hear about us from others who have stayed here.'

'Hear!'

'Yes. And I'll do my best to get the word going. That new telephone will start ringing soon.' Alan left her domain, and marched up the curved main staircase. The mural on the landing set his teeth on edge. He should persuade Molly to have it painted over. It was too sweet and inane, and such a pointless repetitive illustration. Why have a scene – a real landscape visible from the side of the house – repeated inside? It was foolish. Fanciful. Pointless, in this practical age of post-war reality. Everyone had to become practical, hands-on, realistic about what had to be done to recover after such a disastrous impact the war had on civilian populations.

And the Forces had a role to play in showing people how to be practical. They needed concrete outcomes. No frills, no fripperies. Straight, down-the-line thinking would raise Malta from struggling naval base – reeling after so much bombing – to popular, thriving Mediterranean resort. He could see it. The Forces could make it happen. And he and Molly would privately gain. Having their own guesthouse would be magic. Lucrative and sensible. Sensible.

Alan stood on the landing, and regarded the mural. Bah. A pot of thick white paint and a wide brush would cover it in an hour. He looked down at his perfect civilian suit, his glossy shoes, the straight creases in his trousers, the cigarette clamped between two erect fingers. Someone else would have to do it. He doubted there was a ladder high enough in the house. There was no one in the so-called servants' quarters. It was abandoned, and would eventually make excellent guest rooms for holidaymakers from England. It would all work.

He would get a man from the fishing village to paint this scene over. Bring his own ladder. Give him a pound or two for his efforts. Yes. He exhaled cigarette smoke and squinted at it again.

This afternoon, he would visit Commander Shaw and his wife at their place in Mdina, and see how they were running their little hotel. It would not take that long to get there in the motorcar. There were management details he had to get right. This place would have to be run like a tight ship, and the experience of others was valuable. Priceless. The Shaws would tell him what to do, what to watch out for, how to get clients. No Molly-style guesswork. It would be exciting, all that money. It gave him a shiver.

'How could you think of destroying it?'

'It's stupid and repetitive. Look – if I turn and take a few paces, the *real* view is right there. The *actual* outlook ... panorama... call it what you like.' Did she not understand?

'How dare you? This is my time. My mural. My house.'

He turned at the words. It was not like Molly to be so adamant.

It was not Molly. The woman who stood there was tall, enormous, and occupied so much space on the landing Alan had to take several steps backward. She glowed, incandescent, white, like one of the new lightbulbs installed over the kitchen benches.

'*Jesus!* What ... where did you spring from?'

'I have seen your intentions.'

For once, Alan felt passive, cowed by a presence somehow more authoritative than his. This woman had power, of the kind he always wanted for himself. He could strut around and order Molly about, and know she gave as good as she got, but this woman here? It was different at the base, where the men waited to glimpse a chink in his armour, a gap in his delivery, to pounce. This was different. It felt different. 'What intentions?'

'Do not be foolish. Do not attempt to change things. No paint. No paint!'

A prickling sensation of fear moved Alan. His hands and feet went suddenly quite numb and unresponsive. He remembered what fear was like. Flying over Malta in the last year of the war had taught him what fear was all about. He brushed past her and lightly skipped down the stairs, keys and coins jingling rhythmically in his pocket.

In the kitchen, Molly was counting forks and knives. 'Do you think ...?' One look at Alan's face made her stop. 'What happened?'

'Who's that woman at the top of the stairs? I thought we said you wouldn't employ anyone until we knew how much money we'd have to ...'

She placed a fist on either hip and stared at him. '*Employ?*'

'Who is she then?'

'Alan – get rid of her. It's probably some nosy parker from the village down the road. Look – I'll do it. How can they just walk in here like they own it?' She marched angrily past him and looked up from the hallway. 'Hello – anyone there?' Her breathing was audible in the wide space. 'See? No one there. Nosy parkers, Alan. We just have to watch for them.'

'I'm going down to the village to find some helping hands. Big strong men.'

'Oh good.' She agreed immediately for once. 'I want that dresser taken down to the cellar. There's so much room down there.'

'Molly, how will it ever go down those tight winding steps? Think!'

'It comes apart into three sections, and anyway – the whole top thing comes off ... the hutch. Easy!'

He sighed. 'All right, all right. But ... don't stand it anywhere it will block the light. It's gloomy down there. Where on earth are you going to get them to put it? It's huge.'

'There's a useless hollow in the wall...'

'A niche, Molly – a *niche*.'

'Let's be practical.' Molly knew exactly the

words to use to persuade Allan. 'It'll hide the useless niche and store all our kitchen linen ... and things.'

'We need lighting down there.'

'Didn't the men just run wiring and all that to the cellar?'

'Oh yes. To the first room. The back will be good for shelves of preserves and a decent wine rack.'

'One day!'

'Hm. One day soon.'

*

Twenty-one

Whitewash

Charl Emmaus, the wily agent with the too-high heels, had a metal ballpoint pen she handled like a majorette's baton. It flashed in the light when she twirled it, twinkled when she placed its end near her perfect teeth.

Philip Falzon watched her go through her paces. It was fascinating to see how seamless her make-up was, how well thought-out all her gestures and poses were. She patted her hair, sat forward – especially when she spoke about money – and smiled. Did that splendid smile ever reach her eyes? Philip watched her, and felt Meg's fascination too. His wife sat by his side but he did not dare look sideways to watch her enthrallment, in case their eyes met and they betrayed their captivation, or worse, their humour. If they merely shared a knowing smile, it would be embarrassing.

He admired Charl, admired the guts and determination – not to mention skill – such a person displayed in the ability to be exactly who they chose to be.

Being who the world thought you were was easy. He had done it all his life. Being who you wanted to be? First one had to determine what that was.

Considering this as he sat there, at a café table in Marsaxlokk, he looked out at the colourful bay, whose bobbing fishing boats and pleasure craft presented a scene straight out of a holiday brochure. Electing who to be, how to appear to others, what role to play, no matter how complex or varied, was something he might not be capable or skilled enough to carry off.

What did Meg think? He could not possibly gauge her opinion, but surely she saw that choice and ability had come together perfectly in Charl Emmaus, no matter how pecuniary her interests.

'So you really are interested. This is wonderful. The property belongs to a family, not just one person. You might have an understanding of this ... I don't know how much you know. Families of siblings, and sometimes cousins, or the collected grandchildren of siblings, sometimes own properties together. So it becomes complicated to sell, since getting them to agree to anything, let alone a price, can be a bit tricky.' She laughed. 'To find them all, even, is problematical.'

'Is there some way we can examine the site properly, to make our decision ... you see, we want to be really sure before we make an offer.' Meg sat forward and gazed at Charl. Then she looked at Philip. 'Isn't that right, Philip?'

'Yes. I've always felt it's trespassing to go anywhere further than the road.'

The pen flashed. 'Feel free to explore. There are several owners. Nine, to be exact. Many are overseas. Two in different states of Australia, one in Canada, and another in the Philippines.'

'Goodness – how will ...?'

'The notary who has all their powers of attorney can act on their behalf. But he is overseas too, right now.' Her broad smile was infectious. 'So you see, this might take some time.' She sipped through a colourful straw without lowering her eyes, which snapped from Philip's face to his wife's and back. 'I must also obtain their exact asking price, and ... and there are two or three real estate agents who are quite interested in getting a deal, so I suggest ... how shall I put this?'

'We must keep this to ourselves.' Meg knew what Charl Emmaus meant.

'Exactly. Discretion might bring us a *really* good price.'

It took much longer for Philip and Meg to decide what to do. It was obvious from the outset there would be no competing buyer, no opposition to their offer of purchase. While everything was being decided, they took a brief trip to Sicily, simply to have a break, discuss their madcap plans again, and get the passport stamps that would extend their stay.

'We'll really need to get proper visa extensions at some point.'

Philip nodded. 'I've spoken to someone at the Australian High Commission on the phone. It shouldn't be too hard if we plan to stay, buy a property, and do business on the island. It's just what they want, right now. The Maltese government opens its arms to people just like us, Meg.'

'I don't doubt it for a minute. I still get the strange feeling sometimes it's all going a bit too fast.'

'Isn't fast better?'

'Even the children said they'd come and help out during semester break. Everything seems to conspire for us to get that house.' Meg walked on, down the main shopping centre of Catania, neither looking at nor really interested in the wares. Not even the prospect of a visit to the volcano cheered her up. 'I'm just looking forward to going back, that's all.'

'What – home to Melbourne?'

She stopped, gazed into a shop window full of jewellery made with Sicilian coral. 'No – back to the house in Malta. The house, Philip. The house.'

Returning to the house, however, did not bring Meg out of her despondent mood. Even meeting Tony outside, this time at the end of the day, with the sun setting over clumps of prickly pear, carob trees, and rubble walls did not seem to lift her spirits. Reluctant to enter the ruin, they walked with the man down to the seafront.

'No visits with a ladder anymore, eh?' He gave a hoarse belly laugh.

'Tell us what you remember about more recent occupants, Tony.'

Finally sitting around a small metal pavement table, clasping a beer, the local man opened up. 'Well

– they say that whenever anyone tried to renovate or repair, the house returned to its ruined state, overnight. Ha ha – like magic.'

'Really?'

'Yes, workmen would return in the morning to find they had to redo yesterday's work. You know – window frames, balcony railings ... that sort of thing. They would vanish by morning. I don't believe in ghosts, but that is ... look, someone else might explain it better than me.'

'Local thieves?'

'In Marsaxlokk? This is a small place – but it's not that impossible, I suppose.'

'I've spoken to Jessie, at the little shop behind the church. Her great grandmother was a seamstress who visited the house.'

The large man shivered. 'Ugh. Measuring up the white lady for a new silk dress.'

'Now why a *white* lady?' Meg was intrigued.

The Maltese man's hand paused on the way to his mouth with the beer glass suspended in mid-air. It shook slightly. 'I thought all female ghosts wear a white dress ... you know, like a bride. There's one in Verdala Palace. People see her at the ball of the August Moon, every year. Someone sees her *every* year. In white. Um – or blue. Some also say she wears blue – but I've never seen her, so how could I know? It was a lady who threw herself off the battlements of the castle. She was unhappily married.'

'Are there more?'

Tony gave Meg a look that emphasized his words. 'Naturally. Naturally. Don't you have ghosts in Australia?'

Philip smiled. 'A few.'

'There was a white lady at Msida, at Villa Fleri. That was a bride too, married off to someone who ... what did he do? Behead her, I think. I can't remember, but she used to scare the wits out of kids who trespassed when the house was abandoned.' He sipped his beer and swallowed. 'There's one in Mdina.'

'The ancient walled city.'

'Yes – that's one white lady only men can see. And boys. It's the soul of a woman whose father married her off to a count. She had another suitor who became so jealous he killed her. That one is a gentle ghost.'

'Gentle!'

'She gives good advice.'

Meg could not help smiling. 'Really.'

Tony nodded. 'You don't believe this. You're ... what's that word?'

'Sceptical.'

'Something like that. So you are the perfect people to buy the place, see? A ghost would be unwilling to play tricks on such a determined ... um, sceptical couple. Such unshakeable willpower is difficult to fight. She will ... well, I think she will help, not hinder, you know?'

They nodded together.

'At one point it was a bordello – sorry, but it's true. This was after the war. And many many men drove away in a hurry, because she appeared on the stairs. Some people say there is a painted wall up the stairs, you know, a fresco, and she comes right out of the painted wall in her white dress. And a veil – a veil over her face. Now if I saw something like that, I would drive away in a hurry too.'

'Have you ever seen or heard anything, Tony? You've been in there.' Philip felt uneasy. Suddenly his stomach started to shrink. The beer was not agreeing with him.

'Never after dark – do you think I'm stupid? I know that place, but I've never seen a ghost. Or a picture painted on a wall.'

'What?' Philip had a distinct memory of a mural. He came close to mentioning it, but stopped when Meg asked the waiter for a menu.

'We have heard the bell, but.' The Maltese man

nodded. 'We all have. If you live around here, you hear the bell when the wind comes from a certain direction. *Mill-punent.*'

'What's that?'

'*Punent* is West.' He extended his arm and pointed. 'When the wind comes from over the fields and the land, see? Not from the water. When it's a high wind, the bell rings. Once. Once every now and then. That's when you stay inside, no matter what. Everyone down this road knows that. We stay inside.'

'You do?'

'Like we stay inside whenever we hear of earthquakes in Sicily.'

'Do you feel them here?'

The man laid his hands flat on the table. 'Let me tell you something. A hundred years ago ... about a hundred years, just after Christmas ...'

'Nineteen ten?'

'Nineteen oh-eight, my father used to say. There was a disaster in Messina. A big earthquake. And it sent a huge wave this way.'

'A tidal wave.'

'No tides, in the Mediterranean, Philip – but yes, you get my meaning. It was ...' He stood, and held his hand high above his head. Four metres? Fourteen feet? Four yards? Something with a four in it. The wave came up as far as the house. It brought with it rocks, torn off the ones near the sea. It brought sand and seaweed, and pebbles, and fish ... up to the dark house. There was no one there at the time. The people from Valletta came, and they had to clean mud out of the hallway. It was *terrific.*'

'Goodness.'

'And did the bell ring? Yes – it was still there, hanging. No one in the house, and the bell rang. I tell you no lie. My father used to tell the story. And he used to hear it when the wind was from the *tramuntana.*' He looked at Meg's frown. 'Tramuntana is north. That's when the bell rings too.'

'The bell's gone, Tony. All that's left is half a stone arch, like the one at St Clement's church.'

'But it rings. I've heard it. You noticed the similarity, eh? Cannot be the same architect, because that church was built hundreds of years before. The man who had that church built ... now that was a man. No ghosts at St Clements.' He raised his head and one vertical finger. 'Getting dark, and feel that wind? I'm heading home.'

'You're a fount of information, Tony.'

'Marsaxlokk has many stories, Philip – goodnight!'

Philip and Meg walked back to the car they parked next to the old house.

'Do you have the keys?' Meg held out her hand, and Philip walked round the car to the passenger side. Pulling out the keys made an unusual noise, and he looked at the ground to see if he had dropped a coin.

The tar looked gluey and was still warm from the sun. He placed a hand on the surface, and yes, it was warm, from a day's sunshine, drumming down and softening the surfacing. He smelled tar, molten tar, and a hint of something else, a sharp scent, a combination of scents that came through the railings, whose spearheads sent long shadows along the dark road to the other side; shadows thrown by the brilliant light of lamps in the hallway behind the small portico. Was it an invitation to enter? He looked through glass doors, one of which stood slightly open. He shivered.

'The wind is from the west,' someone said in the dark. 'Let's do this quickly.'

'Do what?' Philip was nonplussed.

'Don't just stand there. Come and give me a hand. I've brought everything down on my own, after all.'

The hallway was brilliant with light. On the gleaming patterned floor a host of crates and boxes were stacked, all made of wood, all carefully piled, ready to be taken elsewhere. The man who stood there, in old pinstripe trousers and an unbuttoned waistcoat which did not match, beckoned. 'Take that end. This is the biggest one. Where have you been? It's dark and there's going to be a storm, by the sound of it.'

Philip shivered again. He nodded.

They carried all the boxes and crates to the back of the house, and stacked them at the top of the winding steps that led downward into darkness.

'I'll go down and light a couple of lamps. You bring the last small box. With any luck this job will be over by ten.'

By the time Philip brought the last box from the hall, light glowed upward from the cellar. 'Come on!' The man shouted up, and together, they took down all boxes and crates, of such a variety of sizes and weights that Philip's curiosity could no longer be curbed.

'What's in this one, then?'

'Books.'

'What's in that big one? It was the devil to bring down that funnel of a stairway.'

'Are you mad, mentioning the devil? Bite your tongue!' The man crossed himself. 'What's got into you today? You helped me crate the harp yourself. You banged nails into the lid, didn't you – or has your memory suddenly gone?'

Philip bit his tongue.

They carried everything through the first room and down a shallow flight of steps under a coved tunnel into a larger space, then walked together, bearing boxes between them, through a third doorway that led into a room with no other exits or entries. It was already full of stacked containers of all shapes and sizes. There were what looked like rolled up rugs covered in hessian, sacks of what looked like books, and wooden crates of newspaper-wrapped things.

'What are those?'

'Rosa and I packed all the crockery, vases, crystal and candelabras. Yesterday – it took the whole morning. Where were you, eh? Where are you when we need a hand? Down by the fishing boats, talking to those screaming women? Down at the wine shop, chatting and gossiping?' He spat his questions at Philip, pushed a light crate in with one foot until it found its place, and strode out for the rest.

He returned with a sack, whose neck was tightly bound with twine. He shook his head. 'No,' he said. 'No. This I'll burn. This is not useful to anyone. This ... ugh. Take it up. Leave it at the top of the *garigor*. Near the kitchen. I'll burn it.'

Philip was more curious than ever at the man's disgust. 'What is it?'

'It has no business being stored with everything else.'

'What is it?'

'The clothes she died in, stupid. You don't want them, do you?' The man rubbed his forehead with the back of his hand, pulled himself to his full height, and sighed. Then he uttered a cry of horror so loud at something he saw behind Philip that he reacted by turning, swinging suddenly round.

'Jesus, Mary, Joseph. *Santa Marija. Marija, Marija. Gesù... San ...*'

'What is it?'

'Can't you see? *Oh holy mother ...*'

Philip saw. In the room behind him, just in front of a barred shaft that tunnelled up to the garden, he saw a white shape, that moved suddenly, and showed itself to be female.

She spoke. 'These are all my things.'

The man behind Philip uttered a terrified gasp and ran out. The thundering of his shoes on stone steps was loud in the confined space. He muttered and groaned as he ran.

The white wraith spoke again. 'You are storing all my things.'

'Yes.'

'Just as I told you, good. Now Karist will carry out the final instruction.'

'What is that?'

'Don't be impertinent! He knows what to do. Just do it.'

He could see the shape of the barred air shaft just behind her, through her. How was that possible? Philip shifted toward her and she took a step back, several steps more, and she raised a hand and pointed behind him. He craned his neck and looked at the stacks of boxes inside the last room, and saw what a great deal of paraphernalia must have been in there.

When he turned to look at her, there was nothing and no one but Karist, who stood there with a bucket, spade, and a sack of something. 'Okay. You can go up. Thank you. Rosa will give you refreshment in the kitchen. I can do the rest alone.' He did not look in the least ruffled or scared.

'Are you all right?'

'I'm tired. Aren't I always tired? Don't stand there like you've seen some vision – get out of my way, and I can finish down here.' He turned. 'But wait. One last thing. There's a bucket of rubble at the top of the *garigor*. Just hand it down, will you?'

Philip did as he was told. It was more than just a bucket, and it was heavy, so he was glad to finish his task and get back out on the road, where the moon was up, and he could take a deep breath of fresh air and thank goodness his day was done.

'I think I know what he's going to do. He's going to wall up that last room. He's going to wall all those boxes and crates into that room, whitewash over the doorway, and no one will ever know what's in there.'

He stood in the glow of a lamp post for a while, patting a pocket for a smoke he knew he did not have. One day he would afford to buy cigarettes. One day. He closed his eyes in the stiff west wind and knew there was rain in the air.

'What's wrong, Philip?'

He opened his eyes and the lamplight blinded him for a minute. It came from right ahead of him, brilliant electric light that bathed the road and its boundary walls. 'What?'

'Get in. I'm hungry. With any luck the traffic to Xgħajra won't be so bad.'

Without a word, dazed and disoriented, Philip got into the car and allowed Meg to drive him away. At the car park in Xgħajra, with the sea breeze dying down, he turned to her. 'I know where they put everything.'

'Who? Put what?'

*

Twenty-two

Wooden window frames

Philip knew something had to be done. They could not possibly go on that way. Everything moved so fast, so smoothly. The contract was signed in less time than anyone thought. But every time something was done to the house, it was ruined during the night.

'You are very lucky people.' Charl Emmaus stood before them, in a three-piece suit but without a tie. The open shirt collar made him look Dickensian. Formidable. A bit on the funny side of fabulous, as Meg would say, if he was out of earshot.

Face scrubbed of make-up, thin eyebrows permanently raised, skin gleaming in the light of some office in Valletta, his body movements, his facial expressions were so different when he wore a suit it was difficult for Philip to think straight.

'Why are we lucky, Charl?'

'It went like clockwork, and the house is now yours. Congratulations. It took well under three months, which must be some sort of record.' He laughed. 'What I can't do, and neither can the estate agent, is hand you the keys, because there are none!'

'Now we can start renovations.'

In the time it had taken to arrange taking possession of the house, Philip and Meg had spoken to the children; both together on a conference call which also went very smoothly. They were expecting them both to join them in June. 'You don't have to worry about things here, Mum – we've looked after it all. It will be a semester break with a difference,' one of them said.

'Prepare to get your hands dirty.' Meg had never seemed so happy. Perhaps all they ever needed was an impossible project like this house.

'But Meg – it's like taking a step forward and

three steps back.'

'No it isn't – what are you talking about? The workmen aren't exactly fast, but they're getting it *done*.'

All the tradesmen they talked to, the draftsman and the architect they took round to see the place, all the suppliers of materials and fittings; they all said something different. Philip knew renovating the place was not going to be easy. As well as watch out to avoid being hoodwinked and fleeced, he had to learn a lot as he went. They had never renovated a house, not even in Melbourne, where they knew the systems and how people thought.

Here, on this island, everything was complex, convoluted, complicated beyond belief. The bureaucracy was phenomenal. But some of the people they met were wonderful. Even Charl Emmaus, no matter how she – or he – decided to appear on the day, turned out to be more helpful than some.

'Philip. Look.'

'Oh lord, yes.' He got out of the car, rested his arms on the car top, and looked up at the house. The window-frames that had been installed only two days ago were gone.

Inside, with all the rubble cleared away and workmen installing a new staircase, the place was starting to look good.

'The window frames are gone,' he said to one of the men.

'No, sir. They're still exactly where we put them, stacked at the back, where they can be locked up at night.'

'But they were installed two days ago.'

The man wiped his brow and laughed. 'Your head does the work faster than we can, sir! Ha ha.'

'Hear that, Meg?'

'What?'

'He said the frames are all stacked at the back.'

She smiled. 'Of course they are. What do you

mean?'

Was it not Meg who had just pointed out the frames had disappeared off the windows? Was he hearing things now?

'We can't work very fast on the stairs, sir. Because they were deliberately smashed, very long ago. They didn't just fall down, you know?'

'Really?'

'Yes. Come and see.' The workman showed him how, some time in the remote past, the beautiful curved stone staircase had been demolished, destroyed, purposely and with a specific intention. He put his hand in a hollow, next to a broken tread, to show how it had been sliced with a stone axe. 'When houses have no stairs they cannot be explored, and they cannot be used. More importantly, the rooms cannot be stolen.'

'How can one steal rooms?'

'Well – not here, but when houses are built next to each other, with common walls, it happens. When a house falls empty, neighbours on either side simply break a doorway into a shared wall, and then wall up doorways into the rest of the house. So, that room becomes part of *their* house, see? From the street, everything looks normal.'

'But this house is freestanding.' Philip was grateful for that.

The workman laughed. 'Yes – but someone could easily have squatted in the servants' house next door, you know, and gradually taken over all the house. And you and I know why that didn't happen.'

'Because ...'

'Because of the White Lady. Perhaps she was waiting for you. Ha ha.'

They had cleared all rubble away from the ground floor, and started removing debris from the winding steps leading downward behind the kitchen.

'Do you remember falling down there?'

Meg nodded. She stepped down quickly, but was

soon up again, with a grimace on her face. 'It smells awful down there now, and I heard someone breathing. Panting.'

Philip went pale. 'Good heavens. You too.'

Another builder hurried up. 'Sorry missus – that's my dog down there. He guards my tools and sometimes ... look, I'll clean up after him.'

They allowed the builder half an hour to clean up his dog's mess and tried again. 'Meg, listen. There's a third room somewhere down here. I'm sure of it.'

'How can you be sure?'

'I'm also sure the ... the White Lady is sabotaging this renovation. We've got to ... do you think we can do something about it?'

Meg ventured forward, down the ancient shallow steps to the back room, where some light came through the air shaft. 'You sound like you have an idea, Philip. Out with it.'

'I've got stuff in the car. Tools and things. I got it while you were dressing.'

'Why don't we look for that third room before that? One thing at a time, I think.'

'Well – somewhere around here, there should be a walled-up doorway. I'm sure there is.'

'Hm. How can you be so sure?'

Philip Falzon was not sure of anything, and there was not enough light down there for him to check the walls properly. But there were torches in the car. Along with the other materials he had brought, there were two torches.

'Back in a minute. Don't move a muscle.'

Meg laughed. She wanted to check the large dresser, whose doors she had not opened yet. One of them was jammed shut, and the other just provided a stack of folded kitchen tea towels, as musty and threadbare as they should have been, after decades lying there. She feared spiders, cockroaches, beetles and any other sort of lurking creature, very unsure of what kind of species inhabited the island.

The piece of furniture itself was falling to pieces. Meg was sure a torch would reveal it was riddled with woodworm. It would have to be taken up to be burnt. This was shown to be true when Philip returned with the torches. She shone a bright beam all over the tall dresser, and was rewarded with the sight of festooned cobwebs and wood dust trails and holes that attested to decades' worth of peaceful burrowing by thousands of worms.

'I bet it will fall in a heap if I kick it.'

'Don't kick it. Come and see this.'

Meg moved to his side and saw it was exactly as he said. Someone in the remote past had carefully filled a doorway with masonry, mortared properly, fitted into the rectangle space without leaving a chink. It was rendered roughly, in an attempt to make it resemble the hewn limestone around it, and then whitewashed. If they had not looked carefully, they would have passed it over.

'There's a hammer and chisel in the car. Would you go this time?'

Meg was up the winding steps very fast.

'I will not have my house tampered with.'

A chill descended on the space where he stood. Philip spun round.

'My time. This is my time, and I brook no interference. How dare you allow so much noise, so much disturbance? There is dust everywhere.' She stood just underneath the light shaft. The scent of sandalwood hung about her.

Philip rubbed his nose. His head swam. 'I ... I don't know what to say. I don't know what to call you.' The words, in Italian, came unbidden out of his mouth.

'Address me as *Sinjura*. I am the mistress of the house.' She groaned aloud, as if in pain. A wail erupted and her mouth, open wide, was visible behind the white veil that covered her to the waist. 'But my name is ... Mary.'

'Mary – we are doing only good things to the house, to bring it to its former ...' He shivered.

She groaned and whimpered. 'Don't, don't ... *dare*. Only my mother called me Mary. You cannot restore this house to anything like ... ah! Mama is dead. Papa is dead.'

'The staircase is going to be beautiful once more.'

'Do not dare ...'

'What, Mary? Dare what?'

'You will never displace me! I shall be here until this house is dust. Do you hear? Dust. Until that mural is no more. I watched it being painted. By my father's friend.'

It was as he thought. Just as he thought. Philip knew what to do. He tried to take a deep breath in the fusty freezing air, but his lungs would not inflate. He tried again, and gasped. He bent over and gulped in air. Squeezed tightly shut, his eyes still held the memory of an aura.

'What is it, Philip?' Meg handed him a hammer and chisel. 'You know, I don't think those little tools will do the job. Why don't you ask one of the guys to knock it down – it won't take half as long.'

Philip was dizzy. He needed air, but he took the tools from Meg and made an ineffectual attempt with numb fingers to drive the chisel between stone blocks. 'You're right. This is hopeless.'

'I'll get one of them down here. We can wait and rest in the sun – the garden is a mess, but I can imagine what it might be like when I'm through with it.'

'Really?'

She laughed. 'Come up and see. I'll show you the perfect place for a bower.'

They wandered in the overgrown house garden, and pushed open a rusty gate into a field, which seemed clearer and more open. 'The big gate.'

'What?'

'We must call that our big gate. The big gate.'

'All right!' Meg seemed pleased he was having proprietary feelings about the place. 'And what was that we passed?'

'What's left of the gazebo. Where the keys were found.'

'What keys? Philip – what are you talking *about*?'

Someone shouted in the distance. 'Sir! The stones are down.' It was a call from the house, which brought them hurrying back.

*

Twenty-three

Reconstruction

The room they burst into was full of crates and boxes, dozens of them. They filled almost the entire space, a huge jumble of them, stacked to the low ceiling.

Meg was first to stumble over the pile of rubble created by masonry brought down by a pickaxe and two shovels. 'Oh, my *goodness*!'

'What do you think the boxes contained, Meg?'

'Oh!' She had no idea.

They were all empty, but it was clear they once contained a great deal, some of it fragile, because there was sawdust, and a lot of balled-up newspaper.

Philip looked inside box after box, setting them aside as he went. Some were heavy and well-constructed, others light, put together with a few bent nails.

Meg took a sheet of newspaper and turned it this way and that. Holding it under Philip's torch, she read the date. 'My goodness, nineteen oh-eight.'

'Ages ago.'

'The end of summer of that year, this issue. September. In English! A hundred years old, Philip – a hundred!' She went on scanning the crumpled page. '*The Daily Malta Chronicle.*'

'How fascinating. Keep it.' Philip flattened a few more pages. 'Let's keep them. We might be able to put together a whole issue.'

'Aren't you surprised they're still whole? Why didn't rats and mice get them?'

'No way in. This was like a tomb until we opened it. Shut off from the world.'

Meg read more bits out of the torn and crumpled papers. *'Fewer cases of brucellosis in the British army. A report on the migration of young men from Malta.*

The feast of Santa Marija in Gozo.'

Philip could not understand why the crates were all empty. 'Meg – where did the contents of these boxes go? Where did they finish up?'

'Up in the house, of course. It was all unpacked down here, and ...'

Philip disagreed. 'So why wasn't all this thrown away or burnt? Why wall up a room of rubbish?'

'Oh, I see.' She stood to her full height. 'Um ... was it all stolen, do you think?'

'I think so. Someone ordered all these boxes to be stored securely ... and whoever it was took it all and walled up a room of nothing. But ... why didn't they take everything away so very conveniently packed? Why unpack it all?'

They were both silent for a moment.

'Philip – I don't think we'll ever know.'

'What I do know is that one of us ought to go back to Melbourne to pack up *our* stuff and put it in storage. I know the kids said they looked after things, but we need to do something about the house ... our stuff. Or perhaps arrange to have things sent here? If we're going to be ... Shall we sell our house, or rent it out?'

'Philip! We can't sell our beautiful home. This villa venture could turn out to be a big mistake. Then what?' She lowered her voice. 'Don't you *ever* want to go back to being a doctor?'

He answered her question with another one. 'Are you doing all this ... going along with my madcap ideas ... just to humour me, Meg?'

She laughed. 'Perhaps I was at first. But now I think I'm bitten by the bug. I'm enjoying every minute. Aren't you? What do you really *want*?'

'I'm haunted by this feeling ... I just want you to sit down and listen to everything I've seen and heard in this house.'

She raised her arms and let them drop to her sides. 'I thought you ...'

'I haven't told you all of it, Meg. I see stuff. I *smell* stuff. You know the bell thing up on the roof? Well – I hear it ring.'

'Oh Philip – there is no *bell*.'

'But I hear it. A single clang, and then nothing for a long time. And I think the note is A.'

She sat on a crate and crossed her ankles out in front of her. '*Philip!*'

He needed a beer. He needed to get out of that cellar for some fresh air. 'Let's go down to that café by the sea down at Marsaxlokk.'

They were surprised at how dark it was when they climbed the steps. All the workmen had left. It looked almost tidy. Philip noted how half the reconstruction of the first flight of stairs was done, and treads fanned gently to the right.

'Look at that. Marvellous. They're not fast, those guys, but they can really do it. This place is going to be beautiful. I can just see it furnished, with guests going in and out.'

'What do you mean *see* it?' Meg's tone carried more than just a hint of humour.

Philip laughed. 'Come on – we could both do with a spot of dinner. Let's walk down.'

The road was quiet, and only one car passed them as they proceeded downward. Philip turned when they reached the little row of houses and looked back. 'I'm glad the builders fenced it, Meg – it looks secure now.'

The fence was invisible from where he looked. The house was ablaze with light, which spilled out onto the tarred road. A one-horse garry stood outside the wall, and the railings glimmered.

'Good lord.'

It was a splendid sight, all windows glowing with lamplight, and the gas street lantern a few yards down alight and flickering. There was someone on the colonnaded terrace; a woman, veiled, dressed in white. She looked blankly over the garden at the road.

Philip blinked, shook his head.

'What is it Philip?'

He turned, just as another car zoomed down the road, scattering a few small stones. 'Nothing. Nothing, Meg.' He looked back once more, and there was nothing to see. The house was shrouded in darkness. 'Well – no, not nothing. The house was all lit up, just now. A light at every window. And there was a woman in white on the terrace.'

'There's no floor to the terrace!'

'I know. I know.'

*

Twenty-four

Plastic emulsion paint

Philip was sure the stairs had been finished the previous day; certain that he had gone up with the project manager to see how the landing had been repaired. It had happened again.

'Weren't we up there yesterday?' He pointed up at the end of the curved stairway.

The man laughed. 'We probably wished we could be. Nowhere to stand yet. Tomorrow the new *xorok* will be fitted, and by the weekend, we can call in the tilers. Have you chosen tiles that will suit the building style – I have shown you samples, haven't I?'

'Yes, yes – marble tiles, large ones, with veins of grey, and a patterned border.'

'Well done.' The man seemed pleased. 'It's uncanny how you have understood the style so well – it's almost what they would have had originally.'

'It is.'

The project manager smiled at his confidence. 'I doubt there's anyone alive who remembers the inside of this place in its original state.'

It was four days before Philip could get his expensive ladder up there. He figured out how to fold it into trestle form, and although he did not like the unsteady feeling of standing on it, started painting right away. He made long satisfying strokes with the largest brush he could find.

'What on earth are you doing?' Meg's voice was loud in the hall.

'Painting.'

'There's a whole team of men waiting to do that. Philip – that's probably not the right paint.'

Philip did not turn round, afraid of losing his balance. He dipped the brush in the paint and continued.

'It's a shame, Philip – couldn't we have afforded to have the mural restored?'

He stopped, took a deep breath, and placed the brush on the rim of the paint pot. 'Meg – it's the only way I know to ... to ... stop what I see. What I hear. What I smell.'

'Oh.' Her monosyllable of realization was quieter than before. She came up the stairs and looked up at him. 'Philip – do you really think you can lay the ghost by painting over the mural?'

'Yes.' He sighed. 'We've been plagued by bad luck. The window frames were the wrong size. The new kitchen plumbing didn't work. There were holes in the drawing room floor.'

'Philip!'

'There *were*.'

'We've had a few hiccups. All projects do.'

'The top half of the staircase disappeared.'

She hissed something unintelligible. 'When did that happen, Philip? The stairs are fine.'

'We had to wait an extra week to get up here.'

'Yes – we've had a few delays. Come down and talk to me properly.' She looked at what he had done so far. 'It's too white, too light. Too stark, Philip. It makes the whole landing look cavernous. The architraves will be ... what will they be, a kind of yellow?'

'Yes.'

'Are you coming down?'

'No. I want to finish.'

'Yellow architraves ... so ... let's have cream walls up here. One day we might afford to have another mural.'

'All right, then. I'll continue now – and then let the workmen go over it with your cream paint.'

'Will you finish it today?'

'Oh yes, without a doubt.' But would he? He spilled half the white paint by taking a sideways step too far. 'Damn. It'll take me an hour to wipe it all off the new tiles.'

'New tiles? Philip – they're not down yet. Leave it.'

He wiped his eyes and looked down from the trestle. He could have sworn there were glossy marble tiles underneath when he started. 'See what I mean? It isn't *me*.'

He heard Meg march down the stairs, irritated by his words and anxious to continue dismantling the old dresser in the cellar.

The brush continued giving him long strokes of white paint. He would abandon the ladder in fifteen minutes, and start to paint standing on the landing floor. The top of the rounded mural was gone. He almost regretted painting over the faded foliage, the bower trellis, the distant church bell towers and the blue line of sea. 'There, gone,' he said, but there was no real satisfaction in his voice. What was he doing?

Plastic emulsion paint slopped and swished over the blue wisteria, the white wisteria, the tracery of a climbing rose whose little thorns, now that he stood so close, became visible. It was just like Meg said. It was a pity he had to get rid of it.

Paint always made him want to sneeze. He wiped his itchy nose, whose tip was as cold as ice, with the back of his hand, and the brush fell to the floor with a smack. There was paint on his shoe. 'Damn.'

The wisteria looked so realistic he could put his hand through the fronds. The roses so lifelike he could smell them. He watched as the man standing next to him added shadows. He saw him squeeze more paint onto a huge wooden palette. The smell of linseed oil, of turpentine, entered his lungs like a draught.

'This is perhaps a mundane task. Domestic painting is nothing like portraiture, or the achievement of sacred art.'

Philip felt faint. If he walked to the end of the landing, he could sit on the top stair and recover. His knees were locked and frozen. He tried to take a deep breath, but the smell of sandalwood, the sharp smell of jasmine, clouded his head and blocked his airway. He sank to the floor, just as a door at the other end closed. It caught the white hem of a skirt.

He watched, mesmerized, immobile, shaking with cold, as the door opened again and a young girl tugged at her skirt, freed it, pulled it inside the room, and shut the door with a small thud. *What a beautiful face.* He had to say something. *'Son quasi finito,'* he said. Would she hear?

The door opened a crack. She was listening. Once more his Italian words hung on the landing. 'I'm almost finished.'

'I know,' she replied. 'I know.' She sounded happy, and emerged to stand outside the door. 'You don't look like a worker. You should wear a bowtie, like Papa. It would suit you.'

'I can't tie a bowtie.'

'Tie it perfectly, and it will stay perfect. That's what Mama says to him. It's unseemly to touch your bowtie all the time. It makes men look vain, Mama says.'

He looked at her; such a lovely talkative little girl.

She gave a hesitant look. 'Someone said a boy was coming. Are you helping instead?'

Philip's head swam. Here it was. Here was his chance. He took it. 'He won't be coming after all. I've ... I've made sure of that. I ... I stopped him coming. Someone said he was sick. I'm holding the ladder in his place. I'm afraid *you'll never meet him.*' Here and there. There and here. A sneezing sensation rose behind Philip's nose and eyes. Would it work?

'Oh. Well, goodbye.' The door thudded behind her. This time, her skirt was not caught in it.

It took him a couple of minutes to recover, to feel blood returning to his hands and feet, making them tingle. His breathing returned to normal and a warm placid sensation spread from his spine outward. He then returned with renewed vigour and determination to his task. The wall was completely white inside another thirty minutes.

'Philip? Would you like a coffee? I've poured you one.'

'Come and see, Meg – I'm finished.'

'Oh, well *done*.' She lowered her voice. 'Do you think it's ... um, all okay now, then?'

He smiled at her. 'I really should have done it with dark red background paint, but I think it will do the job, yes.'

'Dark red? I thought we said cream.'

'Cream. Cream, Meg. *Cream.*'

'You just have to come and see what I've found. There's a niche behind that old dresser. I've also figured how they got it down there in the first place, down those narrow steps.' She ran a hand through her hair. 'And your coffee's getting cold.'

She was right about the dresser, and about the niche. The large piece of furniture had been assembled down in the cellar, out of six pieces. Seven if you counted the top of the hutch. Meg had used Philip's hammer and chisel and split them apart, not worrying about breaking pieces off.

'It's going to be burnt, anyway – it's riddled with woodworm.'

'Yes, it is. But look. Look, at this. It was placed right in front of this deep niche in the wall.'

'Well – there was no other place to put it, really.'

'That waitress was right – remember what she said about houses being built on top of ancient caverns and excavations? This cellar was dug out centuries ago. This was probably going to be another tunnel.' He peered inside. 'Hand me that torch.'

'I wouldn't if I were you. Centuries of spiders and ... ugh – one of the men said scorpions ... there are scorpions in places like this.'

'No, no – look at this. There's something big in

here.'

'Bigger than a cockroach? If so, I don't want to know.' She laughed nervously.

'Come and help me.'

She did not move.

Philip had taken hold of whatever was inside the niche and pulled. 'There are two of these flat crates. Uh - unbelievably heavy.' He grunted. 'Come on, give me a hand.'

They were awkward more than heavy. In minutes, they had three objects on the floor of the cellar.

'A triangular crate – the heaviest by far.'

'And a rectangular one.'

'Not empty this time. And another thinner package, all wrapped in a curtain or something.'

'Filthy, Philip – I wouldn't try to unwrap it ...'

But he had already started. What he unwrapped had them stand and stare, speechless.

'It's beautiful.'

'Yes. I don't think it's ever been framed.'

'Philip – it's wonderful. It's amazing – not one woodworm on it. Do you think it's a portrait of a little girl who lived here?'

'And do you think that's one of the rooms of this house behind her? Green – look, all green, with brocade curtains, brocade upholstery, and gilt-framed mirrors.'

'Where? Where can you see gilt-framed mirrors?'

'Um ... I don't know now.' But he knew they were there.

They gazed at the painting.

'Can we keep it?'

'Yes, Meg. We need it. The contract we signed said *with all contents, fittings and chattels*, remember?' Philip crouched down and looked closely at the propped-up painting. 'It's ours.'

'We *need* it?'

'Don't you see who this is, Meg? I've told you about her.'

'But you said the woman you see is scarred and disfigured. Her skin's all pocked and lined.'

Philip felt faint for an instant. 'Phew – where's that coffee?'

'I'll pour you another one – the flask is still warm, I think.'

'This is her, Meg. It's her. It's ... those are her eyes. That's her mouth. This is her before she got like that. This is her as a young girl. This is what ...'

'What?'

'As well as painting over the mural, what we must do is ... Yes. Yes.' He took the mug and sipped. 'Yes.'

Meg waited. She poured herself another cup and sat on the last step of the *garigor*.

'Can you see it? Can you see it?'

'See what, Philip? You're not seeing things again, are you?'

He took the painting up in both hands, and held it at eye level. 'Can you see it in a beautiful specially-made gilt frame? Can you see where we ought to hang it?'

Meg saw. She knew exactly what he meant. She moved up and placed a hand on his shoulder. 'Yes, yes of course. It will hang on the landing wall, in the middle of where the mural was.'

She understood.

'Turning back time, so to speak.'

'Well – we don't know what happ...'

'But I do.' He knew everything. He would turn everything back to before the mural was painted, before smallpox came to the house. She would always be there, on the landing, and never change. 'Oh Meg – this is perfect.'

In one of the other crates, they found the most magnificent Italian harp.

'Do you think this was hers?'

'Without a doubt – can you see it on the landing? Magnificent!'

'And the last box?'

They broke it open and revealed a superb wall clock. It was inlaid and gilded, with a yellowish face.

'It's beautiful.'

'I know what it is. This is priceless, Meg. It's an *Arloġġ tal-Lira.*'

'A what?'

'A pound clock. A lyre clock. And it's definitely no reproduction.'

*

Philip never had another visitation from the woman with the scarred face. Meg will tell anyone who will listen that it was the White Lady who brought them back together after their marriage had hit a rocky strip. Their children, when they arrived at Marsaxlokk from Melbourne, did not believe a single word of any of it, of course.

Author's use of facts

Villa Sans Souci: The abandoned building, which inspired this novel, still stands on the Zejtun road to Marsaxlokk. A very sketchy history of the house, which was built in 1870, is available online. Many photographs of the derelict building exist, in some of which the landing mural is plainly visible.

Marsaxlokk [Pro: Marsa–sh–*lock*] is an ancient fishing village whose name literally means 'southeast harbour'. Its population has always been small (3,500 in 2013). It has a popular fish market, and enjoys a picturesque aspect due to its sheltered bay full of colourful boats.

Għall-erwieħ is a common exclamation of relief, which is similar to *Thank goodness*.

St Clement's Chapel is on the northern limits of Zejtun. It is an ancient seventeenth century construction with various additions and restorations. It has a higher than usual altar because of frequent local floods, the worst of which occurred in the late 1800s. All the wayside chapels mentioned in this narrative exist.

Lazzaro Pisani was a Maltese artist of the nineteenth century, many of whose works still exist. He died in 1932.

Villa Marnisi is a villa among the vineyards, some distance south-west of Villa Sans Souci. The bell at the latter house was intended as an alarm, to alert occupants of the former of any untoward event, such a burglary.

King Edward VII visited Malta in 1903, in the company

of Queen Alexandra, on a Mediterranean cruise that included Gibraltar, on the royal vessel *Victoria and Albert*.

The Messina earthquake of 1908 was felt in Malta, and Marsaxlokk was inundated by a 4-metre tsunami.

A number of **smallpox epidemics** have occurred in Malta, including one in the late 1800s.

There is a particular species of **small bat** in Malta: *Pipistrellus pipistrellus*, which shelters in confined places during the day.

Horse-drawn hearses were still in popular use in Malta until the early 1970s, and are making a comeback.

The Lyre- or Pound-Clock *l-Arloġġ tal-Lira* was an item found in many prominent homes, and is today reproduced by artisans.

Ghosts, particularly a White lady, are part of common Maltese folklore, and hauntings of abandoned houses include Verdala Palace, and houses in the three cities, Valletta, and Mdina. Villa Sans Souci is well-known for being haunted.

The *karrozzin* is a small horse-drawn carriage with widespread use in the 17th and 18th centuries. Today, a ride around sightseeing spots is a popular tourist activity.

The *garigor*, or winding stone staircase, was part of most prominent residences built until the end of the 19th century. It allowed access to all storeys from the rear of the house for servants, and was generally the only access to the rooftop of a house.

The **parish church of Marsaxlokk**, Our Lady of Pompeii, was built around 1860. A brief history is available online.

Zejtun is a large city which evolved from time immemorial from the spread of a number of villages, whose names still live in the local vernacular. It is graced by an unusual number of churches and ancient wayside chapels.

Biggin Hill, in Greater London, England is the location of an RAF Aerodrome which was the base for *Operation Crossbow* V-1 flying bomb defence during World War II. It has also hosted pilot training centres.

Hal-Far and **Ta' Qali** were important RAF-built airfields in Malta. Details of their history and use can be found online.

Scorpions are nocturnal arachnids that hide under stones and in cellars. The Maltese species has very weak poison; the sting is not lethal.

Tomna and *qasba* are ancient Maltese land measures. A tomna is roughly 1 124 sq metres, and a qasba is about two linear metres.

Ħares, fatat and *babaw* are Maltese words for ghost.

Alphonse Hasselmans was an important harpist, composer and transcriber of the mid-19th century. From 1884, he was professor of harp at the *Conservatoire de Paris*.

A species of Maltese owl, the ***Kokka tax-Xagħri*** or Short-eared owl, (*Asio flammeus*), no longer breeds on the island, but used to in the past. It feeds on voles and other field animals, and flies close to the ground in open country, swooping upon prey feet-first.

Tberik is the common name for house-blessing, a traditional practice in Maltese towns and villages, which still takes place annually in each parish.

The Daily Malta Chronicle was a popular island newspaper in English, about which little information is available. It was published between the late 1800s and 1926.

A *remissa* is a front room, similar to a garage, with large double doors and a coved ceiling. Before the advent of the motorcar, it would house beasts of burden, carts, barrels, tools and produce.

An **aspergillum** is a church implement used to disperse or sprinkle holy water.

Ċeklem-ċeklem This Maltese expression, which is equivalent to clip-clop, evokes the combined sound of a horse's hooves and the rattle and clink of the harness.

*

Glossary

In alphabetical order:

Agħlaq ix-xatba warajk [Maltese] Close the gate behind you.
Agħmel qrun [Maltese] Make a horned fist
Ara x'kokka dik! [Maltese] Look – what an owl!
Arloġġ tal-Lira [Maltese] Lyre clock, pound clock
Babaw [Maltese] Ghost
Biskuttini [Maltese] Biscuits
Burdell [Maltese] Brothel
Ċeklem-ċeklem [Maltese] Clip-clop
Commedia dell'Arte [Italian] A form of popular Italian theatre characterized by masked archetypes.
Dak qamar! [Maltese] What a moon!
Domine non sum digno [Latin] Lord, I am not worthy
Egħrqet [Maltese] She drowned
Ejja, ejja [Maltese] Come on
Ex voto [Latin] Votive offering
Festa [Maltese] Feast day
Fuklar [Maltese]
Gabinett [Maltese] Closet
Garigor [Maltese] Narrow winding staircase
Ġesù [Maltese] Jesus
Għadek hawn? [Maltese] Are you still here?
Għadni hawn. [Maltese] I'm still here.

Għall-erwieħ! [Maltese]   Thank goodness. [Literal meaning: For the souls in purgatory.]

Girna [Maltese] Dry-stone hunting shelter

Ħares, fatat [Maltese] Words for ghost

Ħuttab [Maltese] Marriage broker or matchmaker

Il-gaziba [Maltese] The gazebo

Karrozzin [Maltese] Traditional horse-drawn carriage

Kokka tax-Xagħri [Maltese] Xagħri owl

La campana di Papà. [Italian] Father's bell

La Forza del Destino [Italian] The Power of Fate, an opera by Giuseppe Verdi

Mi ricordo di un volto perfetto. [Italian] I remember a perfect face.

Non sale? [Italian] Are you not coming up?

Pastizzi [Maltese] Traditional savoury pastries

Pendlu [Maltese] Pendulum

Pipistrell [Maltese] Bat

Qamar kwinta [Maltese] Full moon

Qisek rajt xi ħares. [Maltese] You look like you've seen a ghost.

Remissa [Maltese]   Stable

Salgo. [Italian] I'm coming up.

Santa Marija [Maltese] Holy Mary

Seħitni xiħadd. [Maltese] Someone has cursed me.

Ser tiċċaqlaq, sinjur? [Maltese] Are you going to move, sir?

Sinjura [Maltese] Mistress, lady

Smajtni? [Maltese] Did you hear what I said?

Son quasi finito [Italian] I've nearly finished

Strumblata [Maltese] Unhinged, deranged

Tal-midħna [Maltese] Of the mill

Tberik [Maltese] House blessing

Tkaħħil [Maltese] Render, plaster

Tomna, qasba, tumolo [Maltese] Ancient land measures

X'ser nagħmel, pipistrell? [Maltese] What shall I do, bat?

Xorok [Maltese] Limestone slabs used for roofing

Żonqor, franka [Maltese] Two textures of quarried limestone

If you enjoyed this historical story, you might like this author's novel *Death in Malta,* which also contains a wealth of Maltese locations, customs, and traditions.

Click on the book cover to have a look.

See all this author's books here.

Printed in Great Britain
by Amazon